DIVINED

THE ORACLE CHRONICLES
BOOK 4

BY

MONI BOYCE

Love Snacks Publishing, LLC

Divined: The Oracle Chronicles © 2019 Shaquana M. Boyce

www.lovesnackspublishing.com

First Edition
ISBN: 978-1-7333937-4-4

Book cover design by: Mallory Rock of Rock Solid Book Design

DIVINED

CHAPTER 1

Eli

"THEY'RE HERE."

Eli looked up at Phaedra, who was blocking out the remainder of the waning light as she stood over him. She reached out her hand and helped pull him to his feet.

It hadn't taken long for any of them to arrive. He felt tremendous appreciation and gratitude to everyone who turned up to help find Willow. Although, he wasn't sure if it was because their relationship with him, or because they'd fallen in love with Willow the minute they met her just like he had. He really didn't care.

Arsenio's quick stride across Arthur's Seat brought them face-to-face in a matter of seconds. The bear of a man pumped his hand up and down. "So sorry to hear about Willow. We came as soon as we got the message. However we can help." Just as he finished, the twins, Lysander and Hadrian, came to flank him on either side.

Hadrian reached out his hand. "Like he said, anything you need, we're here."

Eli shook his hand and when Lysander offered his hand, minus any heartfelt words, he shook his hand too.

For the next fifteen minutes, witches from some of the local covens approached him and pledged to help find Willow. When he saw Anippe and Gamal walking towards him with a tall blonde haired man that resembled Ulrik, he had to blink a few times. As they drew closer, he could see it wasn't Ulrik.

"Anippe." He hugged her. "I hadn't expected you to come." The reason, hung in the air between them.

"He was fond of her..." In an effort to calm the swirling emotions, she drew in a breath and exhaled before continuing. "I do this not only for myself, but for him also." Her glassy eyes held his for a moment.

Gamal stepped forward and clasped his hand. Anippe cleared her throat. "I want to introduce Rolf." The blonde haired man that resembled Ulrik stepped forward. His shoulders were broader than Ulrik. "He is Ulrik's brother."

"The werewolf." It was all that Eli managed to say as he took in the similarities again. He definitely looked like he belonged in the pages of a history book where they discussed Vikings, just like his brother.

"My brother must have trusted you, if he shared that piece of information with you." Rolf's studied gaze was trained on him. He scrutinized him without apology, like he was trying to figure out why Ulrik had trusted him. If the guy was broken up over the loss of his brother, he couldn't tell. Before Eli could say anything further, Rolf lost interest in him, when his eyes landed on Phaedra. "Who are you?"

Most women at this point would have been all blushes and giggles to be under the admiring eyes of a man that looked like Rolf, but Phaedra looked back at him with a disinterested look. "Phaedra."

Max wasted no time in putting his arm around Phaedra and growling low in his throat at Rolf. In an instant, Rolf's relaxed stance went on high alert in the midst of another wolf. If they had been in their dog or werewolf form, both men would have raised hackles. Snarling went back and forth between the two, like they were the only two standing on the hill.

Max would have hell to pay later for the territorial gesture. No one treated Phaedra like she was some prize to be won, a possession or in this case, a bone that two dogs were fighting over.

If it hadn't been for the fact that they were all here to save Willow, he might have enjoyed seeing Rolf and Max fight over Phaedra, if only so he could tease her about it.

He's sure he would even have watched in amusement as Rolf did his best to try and win Phaedra over, only to be met with abuse and her sharp tongue.

"Now that we're all here. Let's get started strategizing about how this should work." Thankfully, that broke the hostility and tension that were brewing between Rolf and Max.

Rolf tore his angry scowl from Max and gave Phaedra another appreciative glance before getting down to business. "I would have brought the rest of my pack with me, but we were in the middle of handling a job. When Anippe called I knew my brother would have been here if he was still alive so I came in his stead."

Despite him riling up Max, he appreciated that Rolf made the trip. He was certainly no Ulrik, who seemed to have manners and chivalry, but he made up for it with two other characteristics his brother had in abundance: honor and loyalty.

Once everyone gathered around, Eli started laying out his plan. "What we know is that Killian's castle is somewhere here in Scotland. We don't even have a hint of a location yet, but that's where all of you come in." He looked around at the sea of eager faces. "More of us, means we can cover more ground. We're trying to hit up all the supernatural factions to see who might have information or know anything. There is bound to be someone that has information on where he is holding Willow. It's imperative we find her. I don't have to tell you all what's at stake if we don't." For the first time since they'd all gathered, the air hung heavy with the grimness of the situation.

If they didn't find Willow, it could mean the end of the world, as they knew it. Once Killian gained control over Willow by turning her or bending her to his will it would be game over.

"Phaedra's going to split you up into groups and assign you a city or area of the country to cover. Each hour, everyone needs to report back here and check in. That way we can cross off places or know if anyone has found out information that may be helpful."

From there, Phaedra took charge and began assigning everyone. People teleported to their destinations once they were given everything they needed.

CHAPTER 2

Willow

"WHAT THE HELL?" Morgana's words were cut short as Willow continued to situate and lodge her soul securely in Morgana's body. Cosmo warned her to expect resistance, and Morgana was doing her best to force her out, but she dug in. "My will... is stronger than yours." She said the words not only to prove to Morgana how serious she was, but also to push herself and will herself to believe that she could triumph over her. If she couldn't take complete possession, she wasn't sure there would be another chance or way to kill Killian.

The only thing working in her favor was that she had taken Morgana by surprise. It was hard to describe what fighting with someone's soul felt like. The only word she could think to describe it was unpleasant. As they dueled for dominance, Morgana's body was like a marionette on a string. It tripped, stumbled and flailed about like it was under the control of some other force. She banged into the mirror, before whirling about and striking Morgana's knee against the bed.

Thankfully, she was quicker than Morgana. She spit out the words of one of the spells Brielle had given her and was able to bind and suppress Morgana, which included her capability to talk. "Attineo hic venefica de effectio magia." The spell abruptly put an end to most of Morgana's struggles. She could tell her use of magic had rendered Morgana dumbfounded. At least she now had some semblance of control over the body and could hopefully get past any guards undetected on the way to Killian.

A frisson of fear traveled up her spine, or rather Morgana's spine. Hopefully, no one had heard all of the crashing around that went on and come to investigate. Revulsion settled in her stomach. She hated being in Morgana's body, given all the awful things she'd done.

Morgana's presence was still keenly felt. Occasionally, her steps jerked or halted as she left Morgana's chamber and walked along the dimly lit hall. Morgana was trying her best to keep her from her goal.

Things began to look familiar the closer she got to Killian's room. Her confidence grew steadily over the lack of obstacles and opponents in her way. *You got this.*

She rounded the corner of the hall that would take her to Killian's room, and saw one of the vampires leaning against the wall reading a magazine. Her confidence plummeted for a second, but then she squared her shoulders and straightened her posture. She had to make this guard believe she was Morgana. It was all in the attitude and haughty nature that Morgana exuded. If she could pull that off, she'd be able to get into Killian's room without any trouble.

The guard looked up from the article he was reading as she approached. She fought the urge to wave or say hello, knowing that Morgana would deem herself above the help. She stuck her nose in the air and didn't even look at him as she spoke. "He's expecting me. We wish to be alone..." Finally, she turned her gaze on him and delivered an icy glare. "Leave." Hopefully, her performance had done the trick. The corner of her mouth quivered. Morgana was trying her best to break through, but the spell was keeping her in check... for now.

His eyebrow narrowed at the tic. She didn't let her eye contact waver as she kept shooting him the best death stare she could muster. "Do I need to tell Killian you disobeyed me?" She placed her hands on her hips to let him know she meant business.

He huffed and stood to his full height. Towering over her, he looked down his nose at her like he wanted to do something. Instead he rolled up his magazine and walked off down the hall.

"Bitch." He flung the word over his shoulder, making it clear he didn't care if she heard him or not. Part of her wanted to break character and agree with him. Morgana was that and more.

She watched him turn the corner before she turned to Killian's bedroom door. Inhaling deeply, she shut her eyes and prepared herself to step inside. After a long exhale, she opened her eyes and pushed the door open.

"What took you so long?"

Her back stiffened when she heard his voice. She'd prayed and hoped he would be asleep when she entered. Dread pooled in her stomach. His voice was dangerously close, like he was standing right next to her. When she'd told the guard he was expecting her, it had been a lie told to gain her entrance. She hadn't considered they would actually be meeting.

The darkness of the room kept her from seeing him right away. His eyes were the first things she saw. She swallowed the scream that clawed its way up the back of her throat. He loomed in the darkness about a foot in front of her. The rest of him came into view as he stepped into her personal space, his naked chest an inch away from crushing her breasts.

Oh my goodness! He knows who I am. He knows it's not Morgana. Her mind panicked, while she remained outwardly calm. Just like she'd done with the guard she kept her gaze locked on his and waited.

In an instant his mouth was on hers. For a minute, she was stunned as his mouth claimed hers in a searing kiss that took and then demanded admittance. Her mouth fell open, but not because she wanted to kiss him back. His tongue forced its way into her mouth and bile rose up the back of her throat. Was he planning to rape her?

Placing her palms against his chest to push him and his greedy mouth away, she went still at his words.

"Morgana..." He whispered the name against her lips, before trailing his tongue to her neck and kissing her there. "Why do you always keep me waiting?"

Killian and Morgana are lovers? Rapidly, she blinked, while her brain processed this new information. That's why Morgana was awake at this hour and had just showered. They must have been keeping the affair a secret as much as possible since Killian had decreed that vampires wouldn't consort with non-vampires. It was already going against his mandate that Morgana was here helping him in the first place.

The placement of her hands on his chest only stoked his desire, and in a swift motion he moved them to the bed. She'd been so caught up in her thoughts she forgot she was touching him. Now she was under him and trying not to vomit. Not only would she give herself away if she puked now, but she'd choke since she was on her back. His ravenous tongue kept assaulting her neck.

Her body was traitorous. A small part of her started to respond to the pleasurable sensations. *It's Killian. The guy who wants us dead, remember?* She tried to remind herself. Suddenly, her hand seized upon Killian's dick like it had found the prize in a scavenger hunt and she was reminded that she currently inhabited Morgana's body. It was Morgana responding to her lover, not her.

'Go away.' She hissed inside her head. There was no way she would let them have sex while she was inside Morgana's body. She turned her head and tried to squirm out from underneath his body.

"What's wrong?" His hand stroked the flesh of Morgana's arm.

"Nothing." She stammered, while her brain sought an excuse. Clearly, Morgana had come to his bedroom for sex, what would be a reason that she would stall the main event? "Uhm..."

He leaned into her, and used his tongue to tickle a spot beneath her ear.

"Uhm... what are we going to do about Willow and getting the information about the Book of Prophecy."

Subtly, she scooted an inch away from him while she waited on his answer.

"Patience." His hands never ceased their quest to remove the nightgown she was wearing.

"Tell me now." She asserted, believing that's what Morgana would do, demand.

His movements came to a halt. The hand that had been mere inches from reaching its goal pulled away. "Do you not believe in my ability to get what I want?" He pulled back to look at her, his eyes discerning and scrutinizing.

She swung her legs over the side of the bed and stood, giving him her back. *That was close.* If he stared into her eyes too long, he might unearth her secret and realize she wasn't Morgana. The woman was just below the surface, still seeking a way out. She wasn't sure how much time she had left before the charade was up. Killian's eyes were glued to her back. If she didn't answer soon he might get up from the bed and force her to face him.

After a reminder that she was playing at being Morgana, she felt bolder. "Of course I do." Reassurance colored her words. She looked over her shoulder at him, trying to play the coquette. "I'm just eager to know what the book says." She was going to leave it at that when she thought stroking his ego might put him back at ease. "Plus, I so want to see you take over everyone and everything... and rule like you're meant to." It was a miracle she didn't choke on the lie. She licked her bottom lip seductively, wetting it. Hopefully, the gesture would remind him of the sex they were supposed to be having.

It had the desired effect. Killian's eyes turned into molten pools of lust. His eyes raked over her ass. "I'll take care of it tomorrow. Now come back to bed." He patted the mattress before beckoning her over with an easy smile.

Turning back to face him, she gifted him with a pleased look and inside she allowed herself a few seconds to freak out before she resigned herself to her fate.

If her plan was going to work, she needed him to drop his guard even further. The only way that would happen is if he was far gone in passion and drunk on ecstasy. There was no way she could bring herself to have sex with Killian, but she had to get damn close, if she stood a chance of killing him.

CHAPTER 3

Eli

"I KNOW YOU'RE frustrated, but we will find her."

Night descended a few hours ago, but they started the search anyway instead of waiting until the next morning. They'd since moved the headquarters of their operations to a tavern owned by a witch in a local coven.

Everyone's nerves were fraught and snapping like rubber bands. Eli's was no exception. He unleashed a frustrated roar and overturned the table. Cups, maps and other items scattered across the floorboards.

So far, four groups of volunteers had returned empty handed and left again to continue the search. Phaedra's reassurances did little to alleviate his worst fears.

Running his fingers through his hair, he stared at the wall.

"Stop your tantrums and clean up the mess you made. No ones going to keep walking on eggshells because you're frustrated and can't control your temper." She scolded him like a child.

Without looking at her, he used magic to repair the damaged table and return the items to the tabletop. "Reconcinno."

Phaedra came and stood beside him. "We will find her." She placed her hand on his shoulder and gave a gentle squeeze.

Zoriana stepped into the room and his cooling anger was rekindled at the sight of her. She avoided his heated look and kept her eyes trained on Phaedra as she delivered an update. "Still nothing. We can cross the Orkney Islands off the list. There was no sign of Killian, any of his minions or traces of a hideout." "We'll cross it off the map. Where will you head next?" Phaedra walked over to the table and crossed out the section of the map that Zoriana's team had searched.

"I'll be heading back out with Anippe and Gamal to search the Outer Hebrides."

"Report back as soon as you can." Phaedra's eyes were on him, as Zoriana left the room. "You should give her a break. If you did then you could hear how sorry she is for the part she played in all of this."

Yes, Zoriana was a grieving mother, but he was still having a hard time excusing her behavior like everyone else had done. "You can scold me for being angry over our inability to find Willow, but you cannot tell me how to feel about this." He clenched his fists and gave Phaedra a hard stare. Anyone else would have backed down, but not her. If it was a fight he wanted, he knew she would oblige, even if it meant things got physical between them. He didn't want that.

Relenting, he turned his attention back to one of the maps on the table. He wasn't ready to give up hope yet that they would find her. When he did find her he was going to shake some sense into her. On the edge of his thoughts he caught a whiff of a 'what if'? What if they got there too late?

Before the idea planted itself in his mind and grew roots and sprouted a trunk with branches, Arsenio lumbered into the room. Both his and Phaedra's head whipped towards him.

"I think we have a clue."

In that moment, he could have kissed the big hairy bear of a man.

"What? Where?" It was hard keeping the hopefulness out of his voice.

"Lysander is holding him at the Berwick coven. The guy's a shifty bastard."

Eli was already out the door. "Take me to him."

Once the three of them were outside, in the back of the tavern, Arsenio grabbed their arms and teleported them to the Berwick coven. They ended up in a stable. A horse whinnied nearby and further down in another stall another one neighed. He wrinkled his nose at the pungent mixture of manure and hay. Silently, they followed Arsenio from the stable.

Even at night, you could see the magnificence of the Berwick coven, which was situated on a sprawling estate. When they left the stable, a large barn came into view on the right and in front of them, across a wide expanse of lawn, sat a gray bricked, three-story, Georgian country house.

The anxiousness he felt made him want to run across the grass and into the house. He dug his fingernails into his palm, attempting to quell the churning in his stomach. Phaedra glanced over at him as they neared the house. He didn't return the look.

Outside the large, modern, black door with a heavy, square iron knocker, waited a red bearded man.

"Hamish." Arsenio said in greeting.

When Hamish produced a key, a keyhole appeared like it did on any coven door when a member of the coven produced a key. He unlocked the door and let them enter, but he did not follow them.

Once the door closed behind them, Arsenio moved ahead across the foyer and through the great room, like he'd been inside the place a million times. They entered a vast dining room, where a long table that could probably seat fifty dominated the space. Plaids and family crests hung on the wall that spoke of the lineage of the coven. Candlelabras holding lit candles sat around the room, casting the room in a warm glow that might have been cozy if they were there for another reason.

Lysander, Max, Rolf and several members of the Berwick clan stood around. The man that was presumed to have answers was seated on a dining room chair, facing the mob of angry, impatient glares, instead of the table.

"His name is Anwir." The head of the Berwick coven, Brodie, he believed was his name, offered up the information.

"How's that boyo, you the one running the show, then?" Anwir shifted to the edge of his seat and immediately turned all of his attention on Eli. "I told them I'd only speak to the man in charge. Would that be you, boyo?" The thick Welsh accent instantly grated on Eli's nerves, along with the fact that the man kept referring to him as a boy. In any other circumstance on any other day, he wouldn't have let the slovenly dressed man that reeked of beer and piss get to him, but it wasn't any other day. Willow was missing and they were running out of time.

Eli dived right in, foregoing any pleasantries or introductions. "Tell us what we want to know. Where do we find Killian's hideout?"

"That's what youse want to know?" The man's red-rimmed eyes that were probably like that from years of insobriety, wandered from person to person as he asked the question.

"Look at him when he's talking to you. He's the one asking the questions." Phaedra's authoritative voice didn't seem to have any affect on the man.

"Are you bad cop then? And he's good cop?" He jerked his thumb in Eli's direction. "Let's forget about the lot of them girly and we can play bad cop all you want, just you and me." Drunkenly, Anwir leered at Phaedra.

Max emitted a growl in the back of his throat and then snarled as he stepped forward. Phaedra was about two seconds from taking Anwir's head off when Eli shoved him back in his seat. Yet he didn't seem fazed that he'd nearly been mauled by a werewolf or pissed off a witch with more power than him. Eli looked over at Arsenio and Lysander. "I thought you guys said this guy had information. This seems like a waste of time."

Lysander stepped forward. "He knows something. We're sure of it. When they checked with Anwir's former coven in Wales, they were told he'd been stripped of his ancestral magic and removed from the coven for consorting with vampires known to be associated with Killian."

That would explain why the man had probably been perpetually drunk the last year or so. He looked at the man again. If there had been nothing and no one to hold onto when he was stripped of his ancestral magic, this could very well be him. The part of him that wanted to commiserate or even show compassion was pushed aside. He hardened his resolve to get the answers he sought. "Tell us what we want to know."

Charged seconds ticked by as they stared each other down.

"Fine. Fine. I'll tell you."

Everyone seemed to lean forward, holding their breath as they anticipated the answer that would finally lead them to Willow.

"Balrannaig... at the end of the loch. That's where his castle sits."

"Take several of the others and go there at once. Stake it out, so we know what we're dealing with before we send everyone there." Brodie issued orders to some of the men in the room.

"We'll go with them." Lysander offered his and Arsenio's services for the scouting mission.

"I'll go as well. See what I can sniff out." Rolf volunteered as well.

"We won't call in the other teams yet, until we know that this is definitely where Willow is being held. Better they keep searching." Phaedra delivered the strategic command and then glanced over in Eli's direction. "Just in case."

He nodded in agreement, too hopeful to speak.

After they left, Eli felt like a weight had been lifted off his shoulders. He clasped his hands behind his head and looked up at the ceiling. *Please let whatever intel came back, show that she was in one piece and unharmed.*

"See. I told you we'd find her." Phaedra grinned.

He let out a long breath and dropped his hands to his sides. All he could do was nod, before he gave her the first smile that had graced his face since Willow went missing.

Some other Berwick coven members led Anwir away to a dungeon or holding cell that was equipped to quell his magic so he couldn't escape. Until they had word from the others how heavily Killian's lair might be fortified and if they would need to call in more reinforcements, all they could do was wait.

Even though they now had a location, it didn't make the waiting any easier. Instead of sitting, he paced. At some point, he was positive he was going to wear a hole in the rug that he was sure was an antique.

"You should eat something." Phaedra broke him from his thoughts.

"I'm okay."

She thrust an apple at him. "Eat."

His stomach gave a loud growl. He wasn't going to argue. When they hadn't known where she was, hunger was the furthest thought from his mind. Now things had changed. He took the apple and bit into it.

Yowling in the foyer shattered the calm. Along with the clattering and scraping of furniture being moved. He shared a look of alarm with Phaedra and Max before they all raced out of the dining room. Two of the Berwick coven members were covered in blood. One of them was screaming the rafters down.

Brodie waved his hand over the poor man's face, "Addormio." The spell effectively silenced the injured witch and put him to sleep

"What happened?" Max asked the question, the three of them were all wondering.

"We were caught unawares. It must have been some of that drunkard's friends." A burly Scottish witch, with the same flaming red hair as Hamish, answered as she tended to her friend.

"There were no vampires there. Just a bunch of witches in a dilapidated castle surrounded by a multitude of spells and booby traps." A few of the deep cuts on Rolf's arms were already healing, thanks to his werewolf ability to heal quickly, as he dropped onto an armchair.

"Willow?" Even though he already knew the answer he had to ask the question anyway.

"No sign of her." Lysander sighed and shook his head.

Someone had already been sent to bring the prisoner back up. A couple minutes later, Anwir was dumped unceremoniously onto the floor. He gathered himself together and brought himself up onto his knees, swaying slightly as he did so. There was no look of remorse. Eli caught the triumphant gleam in his eye that he'd nearly sent some of the men to their death.

In a fit of rage, Eli roughly jerked the man from the floor by the front of his shirt. Their faces were mere inches from each other. "You son of a bitch! Fucking talk! Or so help me, I'll make you." Right now, he wasn't above doing anything he needed to make Anwir talk. He'd gotten good men injured and nearly killed.

Eli was on the verge of using his magic to torture him when the room became bathed in a faint, red glow. Everyone looked towards the window. Eli let go of the man's shirt and he dropped back to the carpet, in a stupor like everyone else. The whole room fell silent, as they all gawked out the window at the now red sky. He'd witnessed a total lunar eclipse before, but this seemed beyond that. The sky was lit in an eerie, reddish hue.

"Super wolf blood moon." Anwir muttered behind him as he stumbled to his feet. All the agitation and snarkiness was drained from his voice, replaced by full-blown fear. "Bad omen." He mumbled to no one in particular, but it got Eli's attention.

"Willow." Eli whispered. After taking another quick glance out the window, he yanked the man towards him. "Bad omen? What do you mean? Tell us where to find Killian's castle." The man must have retreated into whatever bad thoughts plagued him, because he stared at the total lunar eclipse with a vacant expression in his eyes.

"Tell me, damn it!" He smacked the man hard across the face. When that didn't seem to bring him back to reality, he hit the man over and over again. "Tell me!" Finally, the others were pulled from their dazed bewilderment. Some attempted to pull Eli off of him.

He wasn't sure what brought Anwir back, but by the time he was coherent again, Phaedra and Arsenio had a hold of Eli. He shook them off and advanced towards him. "Tell me." He half pleaded.

It must have been fear of the bad omen that loosened his tongue. "Dalkirk. Killian's castle is in Dalkirk. A thick forest surrounds the castle, to mask its location. You can't get there by magic."

CHAPTER 4

Willow

SHE WAS SURE he could feel the slight tremor that shook her body as she straddled him. He gripped her head in his hands and guided her mouth to his. She hoped her eyes expressed the longing she was supposed to feel for him. It was always hard for her eyes to convey a lie. The truth so easily escaped out of their depths. Since they were Morgana's lying, traitorous eyes it shouldn't be terribly hard. After all, Morgana was the ultimate liar.

How Morgana could feel anything for this monster was revolting. But, when you were a monster too, it must have been easy to be attracted to him. Her breasts pressed against his cold, hard, naked chest. As she straddled him, she became aware that he wore only pajama bottoms and no underwear. His erection was rubbing against all the wrong places.

Again, she suppressed the urge to dry heave or vomit, while his tongue snaked around, exploring every crevice and hollow of Morgana's mouth.

Just when she thought she couldn't take anymore, the moonlight in the room shifted to an eerie red. She broke away from the kiss and looked out the window. The eclipse was no coincidence. She'd seen it in the vision when she was out in the woods. Except she wasn't running around the woods right now, she was here in Killian's castle. Another prophecy was coming true. She just wasn't sure if the ominous red sky was a sign of her impending doom or if it would mark her victory over the monster that lay beneath her.

"Isn't it beautiful?" His hands continued to caress her, if you could call it that. His touch made her skin crawl. He would find the beauty in a blood red sky. When she looked back at him, for a moment she wondered if Killian weren't the big, bad, wicked, bloodthirsty, egomaniacal vampire trying to control her, would she have found him attractive? She shook away the thought, as she felt Morgana trying once again to free herself.

If she prolonged it anymore, she would end up having to have sex with Killian and she was not prepared to have sex with the man that had been the author of her misery for so long. Plus, she ran the risk that Morgana might escape.

Okay. It's now or never. The spell mentioned that she needed the vampire's blood for the spell to work. How the hell was she supposed to get it? Killian went back to assaulting her neck again. She was actually a little frightened of him kissing her in that spot. Would he attempt to turn Morgana? Did he feed off of her or anything?

She pulled away and sat up. Her mind was working overtime to find a way to get his blood. "Uhm, I thought we could talk."

"Since when do you want to talk?" A chuckle erupted from him and he reached to pull her down for another kiss.

A thought sprung into her mind. She had no time to think it over and just blurted it out. "Let me taste some of your blood." Her heart was racing so fast she could hear it pounding in her ears. Hopefully, she hadn't just made the biggest mistake. His face had yet to register a reaction, but another part of his anatomy had.

The idea seemed to arouse him. His cock pulsed and throbbed beneath her. She gulped. His face broke into a lecherous grin. "You're going to enjoy it. It's going to heighten your sexual experience." The thought of Morgana drinking his blood had turned his green eyes obsidian. She'd seen his eyes like that once before... in the nightmare where he was feeding on her.

When he raised his wrist to his mouth; his face transformed into his true face. The veins around his eyes became more pronounced and she could see the blood that ran through them. His cheeks became hollowed out and angular. Once his fangs appeared it took all the self-control she had not to scream her head off. Her palms were sweaty and a cold sweat had broken out on her brow. *Pull it together. He's going to bite his wrist, not you.*

He never took his eyes from her as he bit his wrist and raised it up to her like a sacrificial offering. The sickly, metallic scent of it stung her nostrils. There was no way she was getting his blood anywhere near her mouth. If for some reason she didn't make it out of this alive, she wasn't going to die with Killian's blood in her system and come back a vampire.

"Drink." His voice was strained with lust. The black abyss of his eyes stared at her, waiting for her to have her first taste. A few drops dripped onto his chest. "Don't waste it."

His sexual desire had him so distracted. Now was the perfect opportunity. She was so thankful for being a singer at this moment and having to memorize music. It's what helped her keep the spell in her head. She smeared her finger through the blood that trickled from the puncture wound on his wrist and began to chant. "Inficio hic cruor. Exhaurio vis et..." She'd gotten through the first part of the spell before he realized something wasn't quite right.

"What are you saying?" His eyes narrowed on her, but she didn't stop chanting.

"... crour de hic lamia. Verto corpus ad cineresco. Interficio!"

Morgana's rage made her stammer, as she began the chant again. "Inficio... hic... cruor..." She focused and did her best not to feel the waves of fury that Morgana's spirit was sending her way.

"Morgana, what are you doing?" Killian roared.

The poisoning in his blood was beginning to take effect. She was starting to see his veins turn black beneath his skin. He saw it too.

"What have you done? You bitch!" He sat up and grabbed her arms. A murderous rage gripped him.

She swallowed and then continued. Confidence grew within her. "Exhaurio vis et crour de hic lamia. Verto corpus ad cineresco. Interficio!"

Killian lunged for her throat. She nearly toppled backwards to avoid him. Before his teeth could rip out her throat, he began to spew and vomit up blood. He clutched at his throat. Blood ran from his eyes and his ears, dripped from his nose. She said the spell once more while being bathed and splattered in his blood.

Watching him struggle and choke, she felt victorious. She leaned forward to make sure she was in his line of sight. "It's not Morgana, bitch! It's Willow!"

His eyes widened in shock. He peered at her while the blood rising up his throat strangled him.

Even though the spell was going to destroy Killian, it was clear, he wasn't going to leave without giving her a parting gift. His vampire powers may have been draining away, but in a quick motion, he pulled a dagger from beneath his pillow and thrust it into her side. She fell off of his body onto her side. Her fingers gripped the blade. It was like the pole all over again, but the dagger was too short to go through the other side. For a fraction of a second, it felt like her soul wanted to flee, to escape the pain. She anchored herself despite the burning in Morgana's gut, that was starting to spread.

Killian tried to reach out to inflict more damage, but that's when the final part of the spell took effect. It started from his feet and rapidly worked its way up. His body was turning to ash: legs, then torso. Killian opened his mouth wider to scream, but no sound came out. A few seconds later, only his ashes lay on the bed next to her, mingled with the blood that he'd vomited up before being obliterated.

"Oww." She gripped the knife and eased off of the bed. Heavy perspiration dampened her brow as she dragged Morgana's body across the room.

Throwing open the door, she stumbled from the room, clutching her side. Aimlessly she staggered down the hallway. When she turned the corner, that's when she saw the first corpse. The mummified body lay on the ground hunched in on itself, like it had tried to stop what was coming. When she looked closer, she realized it was the vampire guard from earlier that had given her attitude. The magazine clenched in his fist gave away his identity.

Continuing her journey through the castle, she found more mummified corpses of other vampires. The one plus side to being stabbed was that Morgana had gone quiet and still.

When she turned the corner, that's when she was greeted by long, shapely legs, clad in black, latex. Her eyes traveled upward and came to rest on Katana's profile. As always she was stunning and looking fierce in the catsuit. How the hell had she survived when all the other vampires were dead? She hadn't survived Killian, just to get killed by Katana. That would suck. Katana stood over the dead body of one of her fallen comrades.

As if she could read minds, Katana spoke. She did not look in Morgana's direction. "Many years ago, Killian gifted me with my freedom, by finding a way to break our sire bond." Finally, she turned her gaze on Morgana. In true Katana fashion, she was devoid of emotion. She didn't rush to help remove the dagger from Morgana's belly. Of course, if memory served, Morgana and Katana weren't exactly friends. Katana turned back to the corpse. "I've been bound to a man my whole life. First by my father, then by love, next by enslavement and lastly by pledging my allegiance, honor, duty after a promise was kept."

Willow said nothing.

Katana turned away from the corpse and walked towards her, but when Willow was sure she was going to stop and kill her, she kept walking off down the corridor. She'd walked about ten feet, before she called over her shoulder. "By the way, if you're looking for your body, Willow, you're headed in the wrong direction. It's the other way."

Her mouth dropped open as she watched Katana's back disappear around the corner. How had she known it was her? One last look at the corner and she turned around to go in the direction Katana mentioned.

Fifteen minutes later, she was disoriented. Blinking rapidly, several times she tried to clear her mind. Had she been walking in circles? Each hallway looked like the last one. She had to get back to her body, but for some reason she couldn't manage to find her room. Katana said it was in this direction.

If she left Morgana's body, the vengeful warlock would not only come after her, but The Protectors. It was still a possibility that her vision of them all dying by her hand could come true. The only way she could save them was by killing Morgana while she still had possession of her body.

The thought paralyzed her for a moment. It was no longer just Morgana's life-blood spilling from her body that was making her lightheaded. Once she killed Killian she'd had a renewed sense of hope that she would live and suddenly that had been crushed. Tears fell as she mourned the life she wouldn't get to have with Eli. They didn't even have a proper goodbye.

What she did know was that if she was going to die. She didn't want it to be in the castle. Outside. She needed to get outside. Then she could take the dagger and plunge it into Morgana's heart.

If there was someone else here to kill Morgana, she might have the ability and strength to get her soul back to her body, but with her having to do it, that wasn't a possibility.

I just need to rest for a second. So tired. She was in the vast hall that would take her out the front door, but she just couldn't walk one more step. Plopping down on the cold stone floor, she winced as pain shot up her back. She'd rest just for a few minutes.

Her eyelids were getting heavy. She swayed for a second before keeping herself from falling over. After a few minutes, she felt like she could stand again. Before she could push herself to her feet, something or someone crashed through the front door and into the hall.

She lifted up her arm to shield her face. It was light outside. It was morning. The red sky was gone. Had someone come to rescue her or kill her?

Her vision was blurry again. She shook her head, hoping to bring things back into focus when a voice filled with so much anger and hate shouted at her.

"Morgana, I'm going to kill you and Killian."

She knew that voice. "Eli?" She blinked and several feet away stood Eli. Max flanked him on one side in his werewolf form and Phaedra flanked him on his other side. Zoriana stood a ways off, glaring daggers at her. A swarm of witches that included, Evie and Delaney, the newest members of The Protectors streamed into the place.

Briefly she smiled and tried to stand up. "Eli." She called out. In her scramble to get up, awareness found its way around the fog in her brain. Willow stilled. No longer attempting to get up. He called her Morgana. Eli called her the name of the witch they all hated and despised. They're going to kill her. *My soul is in her body and none of them know. Oh shit.*

CHAPTER 5

Eli

MORGANA WAS SITTING in the middle of the foyer covered in blood, with a knife in her gut. Had Willow done that? The hall was littered with bodies. Frantically, he looked around, searching the bodies for her. *None of them are Willow. Where is she?*

All he could focus on was finding out if that was Willow's blood and if she was alive. "Where is Willow?"

They all advanced on her.

"Wait!" She yelled, holding up her hands for them to stop. "I'm not who you think I am."

What game was she playing at?

"If you think we're going to believe that you didn't kill Mathilda, or poison Max with silver, and betray us by joining Killian, and kidnap Willow, you're mistaken, you traitorous bitch." Phaedra spit the words at her.

"That's not... what I meant." Wheezing, she shakily got to her feet.

They really didn't have time for this. If Morgana thought she was going to prolong her sorry excuse for a life she was sorely mistaken. Where the hell was Killian hiding? He'd never taken the vampire for a coward. Where was Katana?

"Where is everyone?" Frustrated, he glanced around the room. He was ready for a fight.

"Dead. I killed them."

Shock stopped him dead in his tracks. Everyone was dead? Tears stung his eyes. Did that include...? Had she...? His fists were clenched so tightly, he was sure his fingernails were piercing the skin and drawing blood. After swallowing back the bile that rose up his throat, he was finally able to force words past his lips. "You... you killed her? You killed... Willow?" Her name stuck in his throat.

If Morgana killed Willow, he was about to end her life right here.

"No." She looked at him aghast, like it wasn't far fetched for them to believe she could have killed Willow.

She's still alive. Shutting his eyes, he released a breath and unclenched his fists. Why the hell was she being so cryptic? "Tell us where Willow is and we'll let you die quickly, which is way more than you deserve." He was tired of the games.

"It's me... Willow." She took a few steps towards him.

Eli took a huge step back, his eyes raked over her body from head to toe. "Stop lying to save yourself. Where is she?" He was hanging onto his patience by a thread.

"I'm telling you the truth. I possessed Morgana's body." She staggered over to the wall and leaned against it for support.

Eli eyed each of the team, trying to figure out if they believed what she was saying. Skepticism colored most of their faces.

She must have seen they didn't believe her, because she spoke again before any of them could say anything. "Cosmo taught me how to possess someone. There's no way Morgana would know about that or Cosmo."

"I'm not buying. What if you just tortured Willow and got that information?" Max had reverted back to his human form when he realized there would be no fight. He scrambled into a pair of pants he'd pulled off one of the corpses as he spoke. His distrustful look spoke volumes. If there were anyone on the team that would have bought her story, it would have been him.

"Nice try. I'm only going to ask once more." For a minute, his gaze turned to one of pity. He did pity Morgana, because if he gave the word, any of them would kill her in a heartbeat or maybe they wanted to give her a slow agonizing death. He wasn't sure and he didn't care. "Where is Willow?"

"I'm trying to tell you. I'm Willow."

He'd had enough. He nodded his head at Phaedra and Max. Each of them grabbed one of her arms and prepared to lead her away to another room and kill her.

"Eli, wait!" With what little strength she had left, Morgana struggled between the two. Her futile attempts to dislodge them were almost comical. "That night when you came in and found me in the middle of a Killian nightmare..." The words came out in a rush. "Do you remember?" Her eyes pleaded with him.

"Hold on a sec."

Phaedra and Max stopped dragging her away, but they didn't release their hold on her. "Go ahead."

A tear slipped down Morgana's cheek. She exhaled a trembling breath. "When I woke up, you ran a bath for us... you scented it with lavender..." She stared into his eyes.

Something inside of him stirred at her words. There was no way Morgana could have known that.

"Do you remember the question you asked me that night?"

He swallowed thickly, unable to speak. *It can't be.*

"I told you I rather liked singing for an audience of one these days."

"Willow..." He looked at Morgana's body, but with different eyes. "It really is you."

She nodded. "Yes, you silly wizard. It's me." She gave him a weak smile as tears cascaded down her cheeks.

"Let her go." He rushed towards her. Her dig at him being a wizard sealed it. The first night he cooked for her at his apartment, before they dragged her away from her life, he'd told her a wizard was a poser and she'd jokingly called him one to try and make him angry.

Without their support, when Phaedra and Max released her, she collapsed. Before she could hit the ground, he caught her. "I'm going to kill Cosmo for teaching you possession and not telling anyone." He was trying to distract himself from worrying. Morgana's face was ghostly white from the blood loss.

She tried to smile. "Don't be mad at Cos— ..." The rest of the sentence went unfinished because she began convulsing.

"Help me." The others moved around Morgana's body and helped him lay her on the ground where she wouldn't cause herself an injury. His heart was in his throat.

Brodie and Rolf approached.

"It looks like everyone is either dead or has fled." Brodie offered the update while he turned concerned eyes on Morgana.

"What can we do to help? Did she tell you where Willow is being held? If she's still here?" Rolf pressed Eli for information.

Morgana stopped seizing, her body going limp and unconscious.

Eli looked at the pair of them. "Willow took possession of Morgana. She's still in there." Worry edged his voice.

"Where's her body?"

"We don't know yet."

Morgana's body moved against him and Eli looked down. Her eyes fluttered open. "We don't have much longer. I can't hold her much longer... I'm tired."

"Where's your body?"

"I couldn't remember... how to get back to the chamber." Her voice was completely fatigued.

"Get everyone to search every room until you locate her body." He turned back to Willow. "Why don't we heal Morgana's body? Then you'll have the strength..."

"No!" She gripped his arm with a strength she shouldn't have been capable of in her condition. "No... you can't do that." She took a deep exhale. "You can't heal her body or she'll have the strength to kick me out..."

She looked around the group at everyone. "I left Walker House to go after Killian and Morgana on my own because I had a vision..." More tears fell from her eyes. She clutched his arm tighter. "I had a vision that she killed all of you."

Shock registered on all of their faces at her admission.

"I had to come alone. I had to do this alone, because I wasn't going to let you die for me."

"But you don't know that for sure. We could have helped." Max grabbed Morgana's hand.

"No, you couldn't. I saw the vision, many different times and no matter how I saw it, if you had all come with me, you died… if you heal her, the vision might still come true." She pushed herself into a sitting position and grabbed onto his arms. Desperation settled in her eyes. "The only way for the vision not to come true is for you to kill her right now." She reached for the dagger protruding from her gut.

Quickly, he grabbed her hands to stop her. "Don't." His eyes took in her face. He opened and closed his mouth, unsure what to say. "I can't."

"You must Eli. If she survives…" She shook her head.

"What about you?" The rest of what he wanted to say, hung in the air. *What about us? I don't want to live without you. Don't leave me.*

"There's a good chance that I can make it out of her body before she dies and get back to my own…" Her red, puffy eyes conveyed what he didn't want to hear before she even said the words, "But… if I don't… at least that means all of you will live." Her lip quivered.

Fuck! It could be the last time he got to speak to Willow and it had to be while she was in Morgana's body. This was grossly unfair. "No. No. There has to be another way."

"There isn't..." She sighed and leaned her forehead against his. "Please do this."

Hearing those whispered words pained him. She didn't know what she was asking of him. If he did what she asked and she died too, he'd be responsible and he couldn't bear it.

"If she wins... if she's able to kill you, any of you, I couldn't live with myself." Her body trembled.

"I'm running... out of... time. Please... I can't fight her much longer."

Phaedra placed her hand on his shoulder. He couldn't bring himself to look at her. Instead he cupped Morgana's face in his hands and kissed her lips. When he pulled back to look at her face, a tear trickled out of the corner of her eye. Why couldn't he be staring into Willow's beautiful brown eyes if this had to be the end? "I love you."

"I love you too." Morgana's soul must have been fighting Willow's for dominance, because the body contorted and she winced in pain. "Do it now." The words were barely above a whisper.

His hand hesitated on the dagger. Their eyes were locked on each other. When he finally made the move to pull the blade from her belly and stab her with it, she gave a swift intake of breath and her eyes took on a funny look. Blood dribbled out of the side of her mouth. When he looked down, the end of a sword protruded from her chest.

Over Morgana's shoulder, he saw Zoriana kneeling behind her. She stared back at him, unrepentant, while she removed the sword and ran Morgana's body through several more times.

Morgana's body pitched forward and her bloody corpse fell into his lap.

"Willow." The ragged whisper hung in the air, like he was waiting for something. After several seconds, he pushed Morgana's body off of his lap and stood. "Have they found her body?" He was doing his best to remain calm.

"We have her." Brodie, Hadrian and Rolf trailed Lysander, who carried Willow's still unconscious body in his arms.

Anxiously, Eli rushed to meet him. He took her from him and cradled her against his body. "Wake up baby. Wake up." He crooned to her, not caring who was around or who heard him. His fingers smoothed her hair out of her face, smearing her cheek in Morgana's blood.

Phaedra grabbed her wrist and checked for a pulse. He watched her face intently, waiting for a sign, a crumb, a nugget of information that would tell him that she was alive. When Phaedra dropped her wrist, she refused to meet his gaze.

"Tell me." He yelled.

She looked him in the eye. " There was no pulse."

"It's just too early. She just needs more time." He reassured himself. "Will take her to Walker house. She just needs more time." There was no world where he was willing to admit that she was dead. He looked down at her sweet face. It looked like she was merely sleeping.

A steely resolve took root. In this moment, his anger was better suited than grief. "Locate the Grimoire and The Book of Prophecy, then burn this place to the ground. I don't want so much as a stone left." After issuing the order he carried Willow's body outside without waiting on any of the others.

CHAPTER 6

Willow

ELI HAD GROWN a full on beard and she rather liked it. She always found him sexy, but the beard made him look so rugged. The t-shirt he wore was water stained in places from giving her a bath. His hair was mussed and looked like he'd been running his hands through it too often. She wanted to mess it up some more. Bedhead and the beard made him a real panty dropper. It was a far cry from the professor look of button down shirts and slacks he wore when they first met.

He sponged the water over her arm. "You look so beautiful today." The words were said with such adoration, they made her feel replete with love.

"I'm going to wash your lovely hair now." He reached across her and picked up a bottle of her coconut-scented shampoo and then using both hands he worked it into her hair.

A girl could get used to this. She liked soaking in the tub and having him pamper her and take care of her.

After he massaged the sweet smelling shampoo into her scalp, he used the handheld shower hose to rinse it out of her hair. He tended to her in companionable silence. Next, adding conditioner through her hair and even detangling. Once he finished he wrapped her hair in a towel, turban style, then lifted her from the tub and wrapped a towel around her. He carried her into the bedroom and laid her on the bed.

Her eyes followed him around the room as he grabbed her body butter off the dresser and came back to the bed. Looking at him gave her such joy.

"What should we do today?" His gaze was focused on her arm, as he massaged the lotion into her damp skin.

She could only hum in response. What they were already doing worked for her. After he finished moisturizing her skin, he placed the talisman bracelet back on her wrist. She admired the piece of jewelry he'd given her during the surprise Nashville date that seemed like it had happened ages ago.

Just as he finished, the doorbell rang. An angry look crossed his face, before he schooled his features and went to answer the door. "I'll be right back." He closed the door when he left the bedroom.

A few seconds later, she heard raised voices. Part of her wanted to stay in the bedroom and avoid whatever was going on out there, but she couldn't. She left the bedroom to see who was fighting with Eli. Who had ruined their perfect day?

"You can't go on like this, Elias." Phaedra was here to rain on their parade and be a Debbie Downer.

Eli paced the floor with his arms folded tightly across his chest. Clearly, he didn't like what she had to say either. "Go on like what? I'm fine. I'm not doing anything wrong." He glared at her before looking back down at the ground and continuing his trek, back and forth, over the same patch of floor.

"This isn't healthy. Everyone is worried about you."

"They don't need to be. I think it's time for you to go." He walked over to the door and opened it.

Phaedra stood in the middle of the living room staring at him with concern.

"We don't want you here." Angrily, he spit out the words and gripped the doorknob, impatient for her to go.

Willow could only stand by and watch.

Slowly, Phaedra walked to the door, but stopped at the threshold. She gently placed her hand on his arm. "Let us bury her. Have a proper goodbye. You're not the only one that misses her you know." She walked out the door without waiting for a response.

Eli slammed the door. "She's not dead!" He yelled at the closed door. His face was beet red as he stomped back into the bedroom. She followed behind him and stood in the doorway while she watched him dress her body.

After three weeks of living as a ghost and still unable to return to her body, her imagination and pretending everything was normal was all she had. If she gave into despair, she might lose herself completely. It was already hard enough to watch him, day in and day out, take care of her lifeless body like she was still in there. They would go for a few days in this bliss bubble they each had concocted for themselves, before someone would show up at the door and attempt to coax him into letting them bury her. She was thankful; he so adamantly believed she was alive. If it wasn't for him, they might have put her in the ground a while ago.

She couldn't even talk to him telepathically to reassure him she was still here. Over the last few weeks she'd watched him look for spells or potions that might wake her up or put her spirit back into her body.

Cosmo had warned her about staying out of her body too long. It didn't help that as Morgana had fought to hold onto her life, she'd tried to keep Willow's spirit there with her, inside her body. By the time she was able to free herself, she hadn't been able to feel that cord that Cosmo had mentioned would tether her to her body. For a while, it had felt like fumbling around in the dark looking for the light switch. When she finally found her body again, she was so weak and days had passed. She was pulled from her brooding.

"Why won't you wake up? Why won't you come back?"

After whoever came to try and talk some sense into him and make him see reason, this happened. He would talk out loud, trying to figure out why she hadn't returned to her body.

"WILLOW?" He tried talking to her inside of her head. He roared in angry frustration when he received no answer.

"I want you here, giving me hell. I need you. I need you to fight. You're a fighter. I need you to fight for us..." He dropped to his knees on the side of the bed and grabbed her hand. "I need you to come back to me, Willow. You're supposed to be my wife." He buried his head in the blanket and gripped her hand tighter.

She couldn't stay here to watch him cry, beg and grovel some more. It ripped her heart out every time he sunk to his knees and pleaded with her. Didn't he know if she could figure out how to get back to her body she would have come back to him a million times already.

Her spirit drifted through the living room that was unkempt, the coffee table was piled high with spell books. Dirty dishes sat on the kitchen counter. She ended up in the empty hallway. She just stood there in the middle and screamed into the void, since she knew no one could hear her.

It was lonely with no one to talk to. She wandered down the hallway, planning to drop in on Max and Phaedra or maybe Evie or Delaney since she didn't know them the way she knew the other Protectors. It always felt like spying when she showed up at their apartments. Phaedra hadn't been lying when she said they were grieving her as well. It was hard enough watching Eli. There was only so much mourning she could take. Maybe the kitchens were a better choice.

"Willow. Willow." Abruptly, she came to a halt. Someone had called her name, like they could hear her. People had said her name before since she'd been out of her body, but it hadn't sounded like this before.

"Hello? Hello?" Her spirit raced down the corridor, trying to find the voice. "Who are you?" It sounded so familiar. "Can you hear me?"

"Willow." The voice sounded closer this time.

Following the voice was taking her to a part of the house she hadn't visited before. She followed the staircase up to a second level and then a third level.

"Willow."

It sounded like it was just on the other side of the door at the end of the hall. She went towards it, but hesitated before going through, unsure what or who she would find on the other side. After a few more seconds, her curiosity won out and she stepped through the door. The room was an attic, filled with old treasures, trinkets, furniture and boxes. Some items were covered in drop cloths other things were covered in a fine layer of dust.

Her jaw dropped on the ground when she turned to the right and saw Mathilda seated on a dusty trunk. "Mathilda?"

She jumped up from the trunk. Excitement etched her face. Both of them jumped up and down, and screamed with glee before running towards each other and hugging. "Is it really you?" Willow couldn't believe she was looking at the young girl.

"Yes... sometimes I come here to check on my mom." The smile on her face died. "I hate to see her so sad."

"Are you a ghost?"

"No, nothing like that. Sometimes the ancestors allow me to come back and see her. She doesn't know I'm there, but it makes me feel better. I think they let me, because I'm so young... and they feel sorry for my life being cut tragically short."

"That's very kind of them." They both sat back down on the trunk. "It's really nice to have someone to talk to that can hear me. I was starting to feel like I was going stir crazy."

Mathilda took her hand in hers. "Willow why haven't you gone back to your body yet?"

To say she was puzzled was an understatement. Her forehead wrinkled in confusion. "What do you mean, 'Why haven't I gone back to my body yet?' Do you think my soul is wandering around by choice?" Defensiveness edged her voice, but she didn't care. Why was Mathilda acting like she wanted to be roaming around without her body?

"I didn't say that to upset you. It's just... the ancestors said you're not dead. You can go back to your body. I just wasn't sure why you hadn't yet."

Willow perked up at this information. "That's good to know. Did the ancestors happen to tell you how I can get back to my body if it's so easy?"

"Remember when Cosmo showed you how to clear your mind and think about being dead?"

Willow stared at her wide-eyed. "How do you know about that?"

Mathilda grinned. "My mother wasn't the only one I dropped in on from time to time."

"I just hope you weren't dropping in on anything you shouldn't see." She narrowed her gaze at the teenager.

"Gross!" Mathilda playfully shoved her. "You think I'd want to see my uncle having sex?" She made a gagging noise and they both laughed.

"Yeah, I almost forgot you guys were related. I should have known better. You have way more class than that." Willow grew serious for a moment. Her eyes dropped to her lap. Her hands grew restless as she thought about her next words. "I'm sorry. I'm so sorry... You might still be alive if it wasn't for me. I should have done more." She looked up into Mathilda's eyes.

"Willow, I don't blame you. It's not your fault." She patted her hand. "If you'd done anything trying to be a hero, it might have been more than me who got killed. None of us knew what Morgana was capable of. Please don't blame yourself. I've made my peace with death."

"Yes, you have. You're very mature. More mature than I was at your age. We all miss you."

"I miss you guys too, but let's get back to why I'm here. I don't have much longer."

Willow gave Mathilda her undivided attention.

"Remember Cosmo told you to clear your mind and think about being dead when you wanted to leave your body to possess someone. Well in this case, it's the opposite. You need to focus on wanting to be alive and back in your body. It's a much harder task than leaving your body."

"Tell me something I don't know." They both chuckled.

"Listen, after everything that happened with Morgana and Killian your soul was damaged and weak. The connection you had to your body when you were trying to get out of Morgana's somehow got severed. You have to spend time meditating and focusing on joining your body again. I don't have to tell you the longer you spend outside of it, the harder it is to get back in it... until it's nearly impossible." Mathilda seemed to hear a voice that Willow could not hear. "I have to go. The ancestors are calling me back. Remember, meditate and focus on being alive, try to touch and feel your body. The more you do those things, the easier it will be to get back in it. I know you won't give up. Eli needs you. They all need you, even Phaedra."

This made them both laugh. Mathilda stood up. "I have to go."

Willow stood up and wrapped her in her arms. "Thank you."

"You're welcome." Mathilda pulled away from her and prepared to leave, but then she stopped and turned back to her. "Do one thing for me."

"Of course. Whatever you need."

"When you're back in your body, tell my mom to stop."

Willow gave Mathilda a puzzled look. "Is she supposed to know what she's stopping?"

"I know my mother is trying to learn black magic so she can bring me back, but tell her not to. She can't and she shouldn't. It won't work like she thinks it will. I won't be me. No one ever comes back as they were..." She shook her head. "Plus, there's a heavy price that has to be made for using such magic. It's not worth it. Let her know I'm at peace and the ancestors are taking care of me just like her and dad asked them to."

Willow nodded. "I'll tell her."

Mathilda hugged her one last time and this time when she turned she slowly vanished until here was nothing left of her.

For a while, she sat there in the attic and thought about Mathilda and what she'd said about her getting back to her body.

As she wandered back down the stairs and through the house to the apartment, she had a new sense of purpose. She wouldn't stop trying, until she was back in her body.

When she arrived, Eli was slumped over the bed asleep. He was still holding her hand. The peace he couldn't find during his waking hours seemed to find him when he slept. The look on his face was so serene. She wondered what he was dreaming about. She moved her hand over his hair, wishing she could really touch it and smooth it off of his forehead.

A short while later, she came around to the other side of the bed and knelt. She looked at her face and silently began to will herself to be alive, to feel touch, to breathe. It was the only thing that filled her mind. Tentatively, she reached out to touch her hand. It did not land, but went through her body.

It's okay. Baby steps. Rome wasn't built in a day. I won't give up until I'm back in my body, until I'm back in his arms. She looked at the top of his sleeping head and smiled a genuine smile.

Over the next few days she practiced and practiced, meditated and ruminated on being a living, breathing being. Most times after spending hours doing this, she would reach out to touch her body and get the same response. Her hand would always fall through her body like a ghostly apparition. She did her best not to get discouraged. She would just pick up and start again.

Then on the fifth day of her focusing all of her time and energy on remembering and willing herself to be alive, she reached out and this time it did not go through. It rested on her hand.

"I did it! I did it! I'm alive. I'm going home!" she pumped her fist in the air. Without waiting another second, she backed away from the bed until there was no room left for her to back up. "Here I come." Putting all of her energy into it, she ran and leapt into her body.

CHAPTER 7

Eli

IT WAS THE good dream again. They were in the meadow. The meadow with the wildflowers he'd trained her in when they were on the road. Instead of staves and meditation, it was just the two of them there having a picnic. She was wearing a sundress that looked incredible on her. The food had been forgotten. They were lying amongst the wildflowers and the fragrance was intoxicating them even further. She kept giggling in between his kisses. Her smile was like a ray of sunshine and he couldn't get enough of it.

As he bent to kiss her once more, he began to be pulled from the dream. Willow, the meadow, the flowers, it all began to fade. No. He fought harder to stay with her there, in the grass, laughing, tasting her skin.

Too late, he was awake. Behind his eyelids was blackness. He refused to open them. The thought of facing yet another day without her, he just couldn't stomach. He'd fallen asleep with his head lying on the side of the bed again, holding her hand. He was going to pay for that later when his body was aching from being contorted all night, but he didn't care.

Squeezing her hand, he sighed. Just another minute here like this and he would get up.

Suddenly, his breath caught in his throat and his body stilled. He had to have imagined that her fingers just moved. It was in his head. *I'm starting to hallucinate because I want her back so badly.*

Slowly, he raised his head and looked first at her face. Her eyes were still closed. There were no other twitches or movement. He looked at her hand; the one he held in his hand, and willed it to move again. It felt like eons that he stared at her hand. Nothing. He was right. He was hallucinating. His heart sank. Shoulders slumped; he stood up in defeat. Just as he was about to take his hand away, her fingers squeezed his. He didn't imagine that, her fingers curled around his.

"Willow?" His eyes went wide in shock. At the sound of her name, her fingers curled even tighter around his.

Excitement poured out of him at her response. "C'mon baby, you can do it! Open up those beautiful, brown eyes!"

Underneath her eyelids, he could make out the rapid movement of her eyes.

"C'mon, Willow! Wake up for me." The last sentence was said in a whisper as he sat on the edge of the bed and leaned further into her.

Gradually, her lips parted, and her mouth opened and closed several times, with no sound escaping. Eventually, a sound was forced out.

"C'mon baby." His eyes were glassy with unshed tears. He clasped her hand tightly between the two of his as he waited.

Her mouth opened and closed a few more times and then, in a scratchy voice, she spoke. "Eli."

"Yes, baby. I'm here." He leaned forward and pressed a kiss to her cheek. His lips lingered there. After he pulled away a few seconds later, her eyes fluttered open. She blinked several times and then turned and looked at him.

Happy tears fell from his eyes as he stared at her with love and adoration. He scooped her up in his arms and cradled her in his lap. He couldn't stop staring into her eyes. "You came back to me."

It took a second, but the muscles that had sat dormant in her face for the last month, finally formed a smile. A tear fell from her eye. Eli dipped his head and gave her a tender kiss. His tears dropped onto her face. When he could bear to pull his lips away from hers again, he gave her the brightest smile. "I'm so damn glad to have you back." His fingers brushed her cheek.

She coughed and cleared her throat. "I'm... I'm glad... to be back." She exhaled from the effort of using her voice after the prolonged period of disuse. Afterward, she beamed at him.

"Please don't let me be dreaming." There was a permanent grin plastered on his face that he was sure wasn't leaving anytime soon.

"You're not." A small giggle followed.

"I've missed that sound." He leaned his forehead against hers and closed his eyes. "I missed you so much."

"I know." Her hand reached up and caressed his cheek. It was the first time since she'd returned to her body that she'd moved her limbs. She wiggled in his arms.

He looked down at her legs.

"Just trying to make sure everything still works." This time they both laughed. When their laughter died down, she gazed at him, drinking in his face. "I watched you everyday. You took such good care of me... thank you." She leaned up and kissed him, pushing her tongue into his mouth.

He was starving to be joined with her. The kiss felt like a first kiss; the way their tongues explored like it was learning every nook and cranny of the other's mouth for the first time. Gently, he laid her back on the bed. He braced himself on his forearms so she wouldn't bear all of his weight. Both of her arms were wrapped around his neck, like she couldn't stand to be parted from him ever again. She moaned into his mouth and the sound caused his cock to jump.

She was completely naked beneath him. He was thankful the only thing he wore was a pair of sweatpants. His hand caressed the column of her throat before sliding down her skin and rubbing his thumb across the nipple of one of her breasts. Their lips parted and she cried out from the sensation. "Please." She begged.

He knew what she wanted. He smiled into her skin and slid his head down until he reached her breasts. He glanced up at her and found her watching him. Her eyes were filled with desire. Placing kisses on the tops of each breast, he never broke eye contact with her. He slid his finger into her mouth and watched her greedily suck on the digit, before he curled his tongue around her nipple and finally sucked it into his mouth. She gave a satisfied groan and continued to suck on his finger.

Willow loved having her nipples sucked. He knew it would arouse her even further. He was eager to be inside of her, but he didn't want to hurt her. With his free hand, he moved it down between their bodies. His fingers parted her folds and found her wet.

She bucked against his hand when he slid a finger inside of her. His other finger popped out of her mouth, and she threw her head back and let out a loud moan.

The sensual sound made him smile into her skin. He slipped his finger back into her mouth. "That feel good, baby?"

She could only nod her head since her mouth was full. It wasn't too long before she began to writhe on his finger. When she settled on his finger and swiveled her hips in circles, he knew she was trying to come. Removing his finger from her mouth, he slid back up to kiss her. He let her fuck his finger for a while longer, as his tongue dominated hers in a kiss.

When she was close to coming, he pulled his finger out of her pussy. "Not like that."

A protest fell from her lips. He sucked the finger clean that had just been inside of her. Lust blazed in her eyes as she watched him. He shoved his sweatpants off his hips and down his thighs. His cock sprang up, happy to be freed from the confines of his pants. Pearly drops of pre-cum glistened on the tip. Her fingers reached up and gripped his swollen member, causing him to suck in a breath. His eyes watched her fingers to see what they were going to do. She swiped at the moisture and he followed her thumb up to her face, where she licked it off. They're eyes met.

He continued to hold her gaze as he lined his cock up to her wet entrance. "Are you ready for me?" He rubbed the head of his cock against her clit. Her wetness coated him.

"Fuck. You're so tight." His cock was only halfway in. He grunted as he slid back out and then slowly pushed back in. It had been so long, and she was so tight. Her pussy pulsed around him, and it felt like pure bliss to feel her surrounding him.

The sex starved part of him wanted to slam home, but the last thing he wanted to do was hurt her. He knew her body needed to get used to him again. Her body had just woken up.

She was gripping his forearms and breathing out through her nose. He curbed his lust and his impatience.

"Did you get bigger?" She looked down at where they were joined and chuckled.

He couldn't help, but laugh too. "Thanks for stroking my ego. Your body just has to get used to me again." It wasn't long before the chuckle turned into another groan. Again, he pulled out and then pushed back inside of her. This time she thrust upward to meet him. He didn't stop until he was seated all the way inside.

Leaning down he kissed her and did his best to remain still and give her time to get used to being full of him. "You okay?" He placed kisses on her forehead, then her cheek and next her chin as he waited. As much as he wanted to move inside of her, he wanted to wait for her verbal response that she was ready for him to make love to her.

She wrapped her legs around him, which allowed him to slide deeper. He slid his arms underneath her and held her. His knees were dug firmly into the mattress. He feathered her brow with more kisses. When she began to thrust herself onto his cock, still he waited for her to tell him she was ready.

"Make love to me, Eli." The demand was said so sweetly it made his balls ache.

He let her pump his cock a few more times, before he started to move inside of her. She was so wet at this point he glided in and out. "Willow." He moaned low in his throat, loving the feeling of being snug inside of her, his balls bouncing against her ass. His strokes were slow and unhurried. Her arms were hooked underneath his and occasionally she dragged her nails down his back when he hit a sweet spot.

His lips claimed hers, and he kissed her passionately as he slowly fucked her. He was in no hurry to come. His plan was to savor her all night and make up for lost time.

It was clear she had other plans. She was pumping and swiveling her hips at a fast pace, as she milked his cock.

"Fuck." The syllables of the word were stretched out as he felt himself on the verge of coming. Her attack on his cock was about to send him over the edge. Using his hips, he pressed her body into the mattress and held her there. "Too quick, baby." He rushed the words out, trying to gain some control over his stiff cock that was ready to burst. Leaning, his forehead against hers, he let out a breath and then kissed her lips.

She wiggled her hips beneath him and gave him an impish grin.

"Stop." He chuckled. "Or I'm gonna come."

When she moved again, he groaned. "Fine. You're gonna get it." He stared at her with a sexy mischievous look. "Hold on." He rose up onto his knees so he was kneeling over her and unwrapped her legs from around his waist. He pushed her legs together and rested her ankles on his shoulder. Wrapping his arms around her legs, to hold her secure, he thrust his hips into her tight honeyed walls. At first his strokes were quick movements that only carried him halfway into her slick channel. After a few of those, he began pounding into her. Pushing balls deep inside of her, and rocking his hips before pulling out until just the tip remained, before he slammed back inside of her and did it again.

Willow clutched the sheets in her fingers and cried out her passion each time he thrust deeply. She squeezed him so deliciously; he knew it was only a matter of time before they both plunged headlong into their climax. Based on the octave of her screams and the way she tightened on him, he knew she was on the verge. "That's right, baby. Milk. My. Cock." The last three words were each punctuated by a hard thrust. "You're about to cum. I can feel it." He sped up and before he knew it, she clenched her belly and let out a loud wail as she came on his cock. Her legs spasmed and shook when her orgasm took over. He kept pumping into her, knowing his own climax was soon to follow.

The moment he came, a loud grunt fell from his lips, and he thrust as deep as he could and shot his load into her. He hadn't come in so long, he kept spilling his seed into her several long seconds. "Mmmm." He threw his head back and shut his eyes, pumping into her a few more times, letting her drain him dry. Afterward, he released her legs and let them fall around his waist. He wasn't ready to pull out yet. A shiver ran up his spine. Willow reached for him and he went willingly, giving her all of his weight. She wrapped her body around him and kissed him hungrily.

Once he was sated with her kisses, he turned them on their sides so they were facing each other. Tucking her head beneath his chin, he cradled her in his arms and shut his eyes. She tossed her leg over his hip and snuggled into him. They both fell asleep without a word. It was some of the best sleep he'd had in the last month.

A few hours later, he awoke to her trailing kisses across his chest. His once hard cock had gone semi-erect during their nap and slipped out of her. He smiled into her hair and hugged her tighter, so glad to wake up and know it wasn't a dream. She was alive. For a while, they just lay together, quietly.

She broke the silence first. "Tell me something." She ran her fingers lightly up and down his arm, her leg still slung over his hip. He couldn't keep his hands off of her either. His hand gently massaged and kneaded her ass before releasing it to rub her upper thigh.

Her nearness drugged him. His voice was drowsy when he answered her.

"Hmm?"

"I don't understand how my body stayed preserved for so long, if my spirit wasn't in it? Why didn't I start decaying? Technically, I was dead, right? Or why wasn't my body emaciated? I mean, I've been without food or water for nearly a month." She stared up at him perplexed.

When he met her gaze, he cleared his throat. "As soon as I got you out of the castle that day. I placed a spell on your body to keep it from physically changing or decomposing. I knew you would come back." His voice was strong and sure when he said the words. He wanted her to believe that there was never a time he doubted. He had some questions of his own. "If you could see me and you were here watching me, why didn't you try and talk to me telepathically? I tried..."

She cut him off. "I know. I'm sorry. I should have told you that I had Cosmo train me in possession and told you all the things to expect. One of which was that if my spirit was outside my body, all communication was cut off until I was either back in my own body or a host body."

His brows knitted together and he narrowed his eyes angrily as he stared off at the wall thinking about how he was going to make Cosmo pay.

"Please don't be upset with Cosmo. Be upset with me. I asked him to teach me. It wasn't his fault." Her soft plea, quelled his anger.

"Promise me you won't do anything else like that again?"

For a moment she stared at him. "You know I can't do that." Her fingers stroked his jaw. "I just want to be honest with you... I didn't do it to hurt you. I was trying to keep you guys safe. I would do it again if I had to."

He appreciated her honesty. "Could you at least discuss it with me first... or at least make sure I know all the information so I don't worry as much?"

"Yes, that I can do." She leaned up and placed a kiss on the side of his mouth.

"Tell me something else. How did you kill Killian? I know from Zoriana that you decided to learn black magic behind my back, even after I told you no." He gave her a semi-angry look. If he was truthful, he wanted to be angry with her, but given how everything turned out, he knew black magic possibly saved her life. Not that he didn't believe in her abilities, given she was part fae, but up against a centuries old vampire, that would have been nearly impossible. He realized the wisdom in her learning it now.

Ignoring his angry look, she answered his question about Killian. "At some point, when they had me locked in my room, I memorized the black magic spells that Brielle gave me. I had my spirit leave my body to go find Morgana so I could possess her. I knew with her being a powerful warlock, it would make the spells I wanted to use against Killian more effective." She looked down at his chest, like there was something interesting on display there as she continued her story. "Once I was in Morgana's body, I found him and repeated the spell over and over again. He stabbed me, but before he could do any more damage the spell worked and finally killed him. The end."

When she looked back up at him, she was trying hard to look innocent and it made him suspicious.

Even if she was in Morgana's body, it sounded too easy. "I'm surprised that he let her, I mean you as Morgana, get that close. Katana or some other vampire wasn't around?"

Willow averted her eyes. Once she did that, he knew there was some piece of the story she was leaving out.

"Willow?" He studied her face intently. "What are you leaving out?" She still wouldn't meet his eyes. "Willow, look at me." He said the words softly.

It took a minute, but she finally looked at him. "Just tell me. What happened?"

She sighed and bit her lip. "I just don't want you to be angry with me."

"Why would I be angry with you?" He rubbed her cheek. "I just got you back."

It was clear, she didn't believe him, because she snorted at him in disbelief. "You will be once I tell you."

He didn't want to do or say anything else that would keep her from talking, so he remained silent. The silence stretched on for several seconds and increased his anxiety. He was about to say something when she finally spoke. "Morgana and Killian were lovers."

"How do you know that?" The incredulity clung to his words, but the minute they were out he knew how she knew and he went stiff. "How do you know that?" This time his voice was gruff, barely holding his anger and hostility in check.

She sensed the change and out rushed the rest of the story. She cupped his face, forcing him to remain looking at her. His eyes skittered away from her face. "Stop. Look at me."

He turned his tortured gaze back to her.

"Just listen okay." Her eyes continued to stare into his as she pled for his understanding.

His only response was not to look away again. It felt like a boulder was sitting on his chest as he waited for her to tell him that she had to sleep with Killian.

"I was hoping he'd be asleep when I got there, but he wasn't. I was even more surprised when he greeted her..." She paused before saying the next words. "With a kiss... before I knew it he had me on the bed." His stomach muscles clenched. He wasn't sure how much more of this he could take. "I was able to keep him from taking things further by getting him talking and eventually telling him I wanted to drink his blood. I needed his blood for the spell. Once he bit his wrist to feed it to me, I said the spell and I've told you what else happened at that point."

"That's all that happened?" The relief he felt was instant. Jealousy wasn't a characteristic that he would use to describe himself, but the thought of Willow having to sleep with Killian, of all people, made him sick and angry.

"That's all, kissing and heavy petting. Trust me, I was just as grossed out as you were, but I needed to survive and get close enough to kill him." She searched his eyes for understanding.

He felt like a dick. She'd been fighting for her life and he almost tried to punish her for it. "I'm sorry for acting like an ass. Forgive me?" He looked at her contrite.

"Of course." She leaned up and kissed him.

He hugged her close to his body, so glad all of the Killian and Morgana business was behind them.

"Shouldn't we let everyone know I'm alive?" For the first time since she'd awoken her smile faltered. "I know that everyone has mourned me, believing me to be dead.

He kissed away the frown lines that formed. "I promise we'll tell them tomorrow." Yes, they needed to tell them, but... He rubbed his cheek against her hair. "Just... just let me be selfish for a little bit longer. I want you all to myself for the night. Once everyone knows you're alive I'll have to share you, and I'm not ready for that yet." Pulling back, he looked at her with a wicked gleam in his eye. "Plus, we have many more rounds to go, before I'm through with you. When he pushed her back against the pillows and assaulted her neck, she let out a whoop of laughter. "Your beard is tickling me."

The tickling and teasing with his tongue stopped and he pulled away to look at her. "Do you not like it?" Uncertainty seeped into his voice.

"Actually..." She peered at him and turned his face this way and that, assessing his facial hair before her face split into a grin. "I just said that to gain the upper hand." She shoved him onto his back and straddled him.

He laughed up into her face and placed his hands on her hips. "Looks like someone's ready for round two."

CHAPTER 8

Willow

THE NEXT AFTERNOON, she sat on the couch in the living room, anxiously awaiting the Protectors knock on the door. She felt like a kid on Christmas morning. The restlessness and fidgeting wouldn't cease.

Eli had made them believe their requested presence was because he was finally ready to give into them.

"Can you sit still for even a minute?" He teased her.

"No." She gave a nervous chuckle and looked at the door and then looked at the clock on the wall. "Shouldn't they be here already? Didn't you tell them noon?" She was about to look at the clock when someone knocked on the door. The giddiness she felt only increased.

Eli put his finger to his lips to quiet her. They both smiled at one another before he motioned her to go into the bedroom. She went into the bedroom and shut the door, but didn't close it all the way. Standing as close as she could against the door, so she could hear, she listened as he let everyone in.

Max's voice was the one she heard first. "You're looking good, man. You're doing the right thing letting us... um, letting us..." He trailed off before his voice could get emotional.

Phaedra picked up where Max left off. "What he's trying to say is that... it's good that you're finally letting us take her and give her a proper service, so everyone can say goodbye and grieve the way they need to." Her somber tone made Willow's heartache.

Zoriana sniffled. "You know this has been hard on all of us."

It was hearing Zoriana holding back her tears that made her realize how wrong this was. It seemed like a fun surprise earlier, but now it seemed cruel. She wasn't going continue to let them think she was dead. She opened the door and stepped into the room.

Max saw her first. His eyes got as wide as saucers. She was about to offer an apology for playing the joke on them, but he rushed across the room and nearly tackled her as he picked her up in his arms and twirled her about. "You're alive!" For a brief moment, she caught a glimpse of the dog that used to greet her wagging its tail excitedly, when she came home from work. Max whooped and howled with glee.

She got caught up in his joy and joined in, smiling and laughing with him. "Yes, I'm alive."

Max finally put her down. When she looked over at Zoriana and Phaedra, both were standing, frozen in place, just gawking at her dumbfounded.

"I'm sorry about... about that." She waved her hand indicating the charade that she and Eli had been putting on. "It seemed like a good idea at the time and then standing behind that door I felt despicable for... I'm sorry." She was shocked when she saw Phaedra dash away a tear. Zoriana crossed the room in quick strides and enveloped her in a crushing hug. She could feel the woman's tears on her shoulder. She hugged her back, just as fiercely.

Once all the tears were out of the way, Willow sat down and told them everything that transpired from the time she left Walker house that night, until she woke up from being dead. During her recounting of everything she could tell that something wasn't right between Eli and Zoriana. She would ask him about it later. She had a sneaking suspicion that it had to do with Zoriana helping her learn black magic.

Hours later, as they were filing out, she placed her hand on Zoriana's shoulder to stop her. "Would you mind staying for a minute? I need to talk to you."

Max and Phaedra left and Eli excused himself to give them privacy. They both sat on the couch. "While I was outside of my body I saw Mathilda."

A sharp intake of breath came from Zoriana. She put her hand over her mouth, trying to stifle the sob that erupted from her throat. Tears clouded her eyes as she tried to speak. "You... you saw... her?" She hiccupped and finally swallowed down her tears so she could speak coherently. "You saw her? How was she?"

To see how affected she was nearly bought Willow to tears. She blinked them away. "She's good, but she did ask me to give you a message." Zoriana's knotted fingers that sat in her lap belied her hopeful expression. "She asked me to tell you to stop trying to learn black magic to bring her back."

Storm clouds instantly gathered in Zoriana's eyes. The defiant look her face took on told Willow that she might not actually stop. She placed a hand over Zoriana's. "Please listen to me. Mathilda was very adamant that you stop. She said it wouldn't work like you hope it will." That seemed to catch Zoriana's attention. Her demeanor changed. Willow pressed on. "She said if you try to bring her back she wouldn't be herself. She won't be the same Mathilda we all knew and loved. Plus, the price of attempting to bring her back would be too heavy and not worth it."

Zoriana's face crumpled at her words and hot tears fell heavy down her cheeks.

"She's at peace. That's what she wanted you to know. The ancestors are looking after her." At this, the keening that shook her body, made Willow take her in her arms. She held Zoriana and let her grief exorcise itself from her body. Maybe knowing that would give her some solace and allow her to start healing. After another half hour of comforting her, Zoriana eventually felt better and left.

Throughout the rest of the day, many of the Walker clan came to pay her a visit and welcome her back among the living. Silas and Josephine came together. Josephine kept doting on her and even Silas exuded warmth, which she hadn't thought him capable of. Evie and Delaney stopped by separately to see her. Archie came by and gave her a brisk hug before leaving as quickly as he came, which made her laugh. Enid, Keeper of Books, even dropped by. She'd never seen the woman outside of the library. When Alistair stopped by and mentioned that Zoriana told him of her conversation with Mathilda, they cried together. She told him that Mathilda was well and that the ancestors were looking after her as requested. It made her feel like part of a family, to have everyone show up for her like that, and family was something she hadn't had in a long while.

After the last of their visitors, Eli closed the door. "Alone at last." He came and sat next to her on the sofa, putting his arm around her and snuggling her closer into his body.

"About you and Zoriana..." She broached the subject knowing he would be irritated at first.

Eli rolled his eyes. "What about me and Zoriana?" He huffed and sat up on the edge of the cushion.

She grabbed his chin and forced him to look at her. "Cut her some slack, okay. Forgive her already." She sighed and dropped her hand onto her lap. "It was my fault anyway. I used her anger and thoughts of revenge to encourage her to help me with learning black magic. If she hadn't been so consumed with grief and retribution, you know she wouldn't have went along with my scheme." When that seemed to fall on deaf ears, she played the family card. "She's your aunt, Eli. It still hasn't been that long since she lost her only child. Don't take away some of the only family she has left." Her words melted away his anger.

His eyes softened and he looked at her. "Okay. I'll go and talk to her tomorrow."

She grinned, before she leaned forward and kissed him. "There's one other thing I need to tell you." She bit her lip and peered at him innocently.

"What?" He grumbled, but his mouth twitched as he tried to suppress a smile.

"Remember when I said everyone was dead at the castle?" Her eyebrows rose in a question.

"Yeah?" He narrowed his eyes at her.

She was sure he was going to hit the roof when she told him. Better to rip off the band-aid than prolong telling him.

"Katana's not dead." She squeezed her eyes shut immediately after saying it and waited for him to rant, scream and yell. When she heard none of that, she popped one eye open and looked at him. A thunderous look clouded his face and she opened the other eye. "Let me explain."

He folded his arms across his chest.

Oh shit. This is serious. "After I killed Killian and I was trying to make it back to my body, I encountered her in the hallway. She was standing over one of the vampire corpses. That's when she told me that Killian had severed their sire bond some time ago, which explained why she didn't die with him like all the others." There was no change in Eli's expression.

"When she saw me she could easily have killed me in that moment since I was already injured and in no condition to battle her... I'm still not sure how she knew I was in Morgana's body, but she did and she let me live. She walked right past me and obviously left the castle before you guys got there if you didn't find her."

He ruminated on what she just said. "Katana's dangerous. I'll reach out to Brodie and have him track her down."

"You're not listening to me. You don't need to do that. She's not a threat."

"How do you know that?" The skepticism that coated his words made her roll her eyes.

"I just do... it was something she said." Her voice trailed off and she thought back on Katana's words, about finally not being bound to a man and finally being free. "Just promise me you'll leave her alone. Let her live her life. Trust me, she's not planning to come after any of us."

He stared into her eyes, pondering her request. "Fine. I'll leave Katana alone."

"Give me your word."

"I give you my word." He said solemnly.

She noticed he still had his arms folded across his chest. "Show me your hands and say the words again."

"What?" He chuckled, but unfolded his arms.

"I'm trying to make sure you weren't crossing any fingers or anything when you said it. Give me your word, again."

He held up his hands, not bothering to hide his amusement. "I give you my word."

"Okay." She grinned and sunk back into the sofa.

"Now I have something for you." He got up from the sofa.

"A surprise?" She scooted to the edge of the sofa again, excited about what he had for her. She watched him open up a cabinet and pull out a book. As he drew closer she could see it was The Book of Prophecy.

He sat it down on the coffee table in front of her. "I put this away for safe keeping, knowing you were going to wake up. Since only me, you and Cora knew your necklace was the key, it was easy to keep people from trying to open it while you were gone."

She placed her hand over the cover. It was hard to believe she was looking at it again, considering everything that had happened for them to attain it.

"Why don't I let you look at it alone. It's been a long day. I'm going to head to bed and you can join me when you're ready." He got up from the couch and kissed her on the top of her head.

He was halfway to the bedroom when a thought occurred to her. "Eli, did they find Morgana's mother's Grimoire in the castle?"

He nodded. "Yeah. The Elders have it hidden somewhere, under lock and key, surrounded by some pretty powerful spells. Only a handful of people know of its location."

She was glad to hear that.

"Goodnight."

"Goodnight." She called out before he shut the door of the bedroom, leaving her to explore the book.

She picked up the heavy tome and sat it in her lap, running her hands over the cover. Remembering the key was around her neck, she reached up and unclasped the snake necklace. She held it at eye level, studying it and wondered how she never knew what it was this whole time.

Her eyes looked at the keyhole on the cover and back at the necklace. *Here goes nothin'.* She grasped the pendant in her fingers and was about to slide it into the lock when the snake contorted itself into the shape of a key and slid into the lock. The lock clicked open and when she slid the key back out it returned to the usual shape.

Slowly, she opened the book and flipped through the pages. Some pages were written in Greek and clearly dated back to the time of the Pythia. She came across dates in the early 1500s, before her ancestors would be made slaves. The late 1600s is where the last entry left off. She went back to the beginning and started randomly selecting some of the prophecies to read. It was hard not to marvel over the fact that one day she would write a prophecy in this book, possibly more than one.

As she turned the page, something in the text of the prophecy caught her eye. She began to read the looped, curling scrawl that decorated the page:

Rekehwer 602 BC

Temple of Amun

(village of Aghurmi in Siwa Oasis)

Egypt

Oracle: Amenirdis

While the Sibyls meditate and await my instructions I wanted to put down the troubling vision I had today.

I'm not sure how far into the future it will happen, but it was revealed to me that a future Oracle will birth a child that could contain a powerful, unspeakable evil that will further spread hatred and division or a force used for good, to heal and unite factions that had once been violently divided. The vision has been shown to me several times and each time there is no definitive conclusion. One thing that is shown is that the Oracle may have to sacrifice this child for the sake of mankind.

The minute Willow finished reading the prophecy a shiver ran up her spine. Involuntarily, her hand went to her stomach. She wasn't even sure why she did it. Quickly, she took her hand away. She wasn't even pregnant. Not wanting to look at any more prophecies tonight, she shut the book with a loud thud. The noise made her jump. *Stop it. You're being jumpy and scared over nothing.* She sat the book on the coffee table and stared at it for a moment. She shook herself out of the daze she found herself in. That prophecy could be talking about any Oracle that could come after her. She turned off the lights and went into the bedroom. Eli was already asleep. After she got ready for bed, she climbed in beside him and curled herself around him, unable to keep the foreboding prophecy out of her dreams.

CHAPTER 9

Eli

WILLOW TOSSED AND turned all night. After the restless sleep she'd had, Eli didn't want to wake her before he left. He wrote her a note, in case she woke up while he was gone.

After what she'd said about Zoriana last night, his conscience had pricked him the moment he woke up. The decision was easily made to make her his first stop this morning so he could clear things up between them. He stood outside his aunt and uncle's door for long minutes before he finally worked up the nerve to knock.

Alistair answered the door. His uncle looked a bit haggard, but offered up an easy smile. "It's good to see you." He ushered him into the apartment and shut the door. Considering he wasn't hostile towards him, he had a feeling that Zoriana had not mentioned the hostility brewing between them, more so the hostility he'd been throwing in her direction. "Can I get you anything?" His uncle was headed into the kitchen.

Looking around the apartment he noticed a wall had been turned into a shrine to Mathilda. Pictures ranging from her birth up until a few months before she died decorated the wall. A small lump formed in his throat, before he averted his gaze.

"I'm okay…" He stuffed his hands into his pockets and rocked back on his heels. "Is Zoriana here?"

Right after he asked the question, Zoriana entered the living room. Alistair was either pretty good at reading his wife or sensed there was something between the two of them. "I think I have some documents in my office I need to go over. Why don't I leave the two of you alone?" He didn't wait for either of them to stop him.

The minute he was gone, Zoriana silently motioned for Eli to take a seat. They both sat on far ends of the couch. Neither of them looked at each other. Minutes passed, before he broke the silence. "Willow told me that she preyed on your… anger, to get you to go along with her in learning black magic."

Zoriana gave a mirthless chuckle. "Willow really has a high opinion of her power of persuasion."

The comment made them laugh for a second.

"Willow didn't coerce me, or bend my arm… I wanted to learn…"

Eli was about to say something when she held up her hand and stopped him. "Please, let me finish."

"I know I was so righteous before when anyone else brought up black magic... including Mathilda..." A flash of pain contorted her face for a brief second. "Then she died and all I wanted to do was use that same black magic that killed her to get my revenge..." She glanced at Eli. "Then it went beyond that... I thought, what if I could use it to bring her back?" She took a stuttering breath.

Inside he recoiled at the idea of her trying to resurrect Mathilda, but said nothing.

"You don't have to worry... Willow talked me out of it."

He let out a breath. "Maybe she really does have powers of persuasion." Both of them laughing again made the mood in the room a little lighter and broke the tension that had been between them.

"I came here to apologize. I was angry and looking for a place to direct my anger when Willow went missing. After finding out about the secret black magic training the two of you were up to, you were an easy target... I'm sorry I blamed you."

"Apology accepted... I'm sorry my judgment was clouded by my emotions." She gave him a rueful grin.

Eli stood up and opened his arms. "Come here." He motioned for her to step into his embrace.

Zoriana stood and walked into his arms.

"You know I'm here if you need anything, right?"

"Yeah, I know." She mumbled into his sleeve. Pulling out of the hug, she tilted her head back to look at him. "Alistair and I really appreciate it."

***

Once Eli left Zoriana, there were a few more things he had to do before he went back to Willow. When he walked into the training room, Cosmo was waiting patiently. The faery still dressed like he was in a cover band for The Doors. Somehow he managed to pull it off.

"I was really glad to hear that Willow is well. Please tell her we can resume her training whenever she would like."

Eli remembered his promise to Willow about not being upset with Cosmo. "I'll let her know…" He stuffed his hands in his pockets and regarded Cosmo for a moment before he spoke again. "I need a favor."

***

When he walked in the door Willow was sitting on the sofa with her legs curled beneath her. The minute she heard him, she leapt from the sofa, ran to him, and jumped into his arms giggling. He caught her, and she wrapped her legs around his waist. Eli was unable to contain the goofy smile he sported over being greeted this way. "A man could get used to this."

Willow cupped his face and gave him a kiss that literally had his toes curling in his shoes. He'd had a clear purpose when he arrived, but her kiss had his brain all fuzzy. All he could manage was kissing her back while he gripped handfuls of her luscious ass and walked them over to the sofa.

When he placed her on the sofa among the throw pillows she kept her legs locked around him, forcing him to stay with her. She didn't need to worry. He wasn't going anywhere.

"Mmmm." She moaned into his mouth before she sucked his bottom lip into her mouth and playfully bit it.

Suddenly, he remembered what he'd planned to do when he returned to her. As much as he wanted to continue this, knowing where it would lead, he kissed her one last time and pulled away. He licked his lip, feeling the tiny indentation where she'd bit him. The impulse to bend her over the sofa and forget everything else was strong.

She ruffled his hair. The way she was looking up at him with her lips plump from their kisses and her eyes glazed over with lust was killing him.

There's no way he could talk to her about anything while he was laying between her thighs. The urge to fuck her was too strong. He wanted to be clearheaded for what he was going to talk with her about. "Sit up." He pulled her to a sitting position and moved so they were now sitting side by side.

"So, what did you want to talk about?" She leaned into him, running her fingers through his hair.

His eyes raked over her face. Earlier, he'd rehearsed what he was going to say, but now that he was looking at her, all he could think was: *She's so damn beautiful.* "I'm so glad that you're back." They were the first words that popped into his head as he stared at her.

Her eyes sparkled and the corner of her mouth lifted into the cutest grin. "I'm glad I'm back too."

Deciding against everything he'd planned to say, he decided to speak from the heart. He took one of her hands in his. "You know that I haven't always been the best with my feelings. At least at the beginning anyways..."

She chuckled. "Standoffish is the word that comes to mind."

"Is that even a word? Did you make that up?" He playfully teased her, enjoying how she liked to mock and make fun of him.

"Oh, it's a word." She said matter of fact as she tried to look serious. They both laughed.

He looked down at his lap and cleared his throat, before looking back at her. "You were the one that made me finally realize that I couldn't compartmentalize my feelings or put them in a box and not deal with them."

"I do recall duty being very important to you when we first met." She continued to tease him good-naturedly.

"True." He mused. Unable to resist her sweet mouth anymore, he leaned forward and kissed her.

When she abruptly pulled away from the kiss, he wondered if he'd done something wrong. He ripped his empty hand out of his pocket, leaving the item in there that he'd reached for.

"I don't feel so well." She scrubbed her hand across her face before dropping it to her stomach. Her eyes shut and she shook her head. "I'm gonna be sick." She rushed to the bathroom.

"Willow?" He went after her, but by the time he got to the bathroom she had the door closed.

On the other side of the door he could hear her throwing up. He tried to open the door, but she'd locked it.

"Go away. I don't want you to see me like this." She whined and began to puke again.

He thought about the times he'd cleaned her up after a violent dream with Killian. He'd seen her much worse. "Willow, I don't care about that. Let me in."

Instead of hearing her unlock the bathroom door, he was met with silence, before it was interrupted by the sounds of her retching again.

"ZORIANA..." He reached out to her telepathically. Right now, she was the closest thing Willow had to a big sister or mother figure.

"EVERYTHING OKAY?" Concern laced her words when she responded.

"IT'S WILLOW... SHE'S SICK, BUT SHE WON'T LET ME HELP HER. WILL YOU COME?"

"OF COURSE. I'LL BE RIGHT THERE."

He paced outside the door, hoping she would open it before Zoriana arrived. When a knock sounded on the front door, he went to answer it. Zoriana stepped inside.

"She felt sick suddenly and rushed to the bathroom. She was vomiting. Now, she's locked herself in the bathroom and won't let me in."

"Okay. I'll go check on her." When Zoriana turned toward the bedroom so she could get to the bathroom where Willow was holed up, Eli followed her.

Zoriana stopped. "Why don't you wait here? She may not open the door if you're with me."

With a deep reluctance he nodded his head in agreement. Zoriana patted his arm. Heavy steps carried him to the sofa. For a minute, he stood there looking at the door to the bedroom, wondering if he should go in there anyway. Hesitantly, he sunk down on the sofa to wait.

It was about half an hour later when Zoriana appeared sans Willow. Eli stood up and gave her a perplexed look. "Where's Willow? What's going on? Is she okay?" It was hard to keep the aggravation from his voice.

Zoriana just grinned at him, despite his panic. "She's fine. You can ask her yourself in a minute when she comes out." She left without saying anything else or offering him any comfort.

He dropped back onto the couch to await Willow. What he really wanted to do was go in there and make her tell him what was wrong so he could help. He folded his arms across his chest and tried not to pout.

Another ten minutes passed and Willow came as far as the bedroom door and peeked out at him. He stood the minute he saw her, but didn't approach her. She'd changed clothes and pulled her mass of curls into a sloppy ponytail. As he watched her, she used the bare toes of her right foot to trace circles onto the wood floor, which she was staring at. She was twisting her fingers into knots. It was making him crazy, but he waited to let her speak first.

Several more seconds ticked by and she finally spoke. "Do you remember when I said I don't mind singing for an audience of one?"

He could only nod his head. *Where is this going? What does this have to do with her locking herself in the bathroom?*

She took a step into the living room. "Well... how do you feel about me singing to an audience of... two?"

"Okay." He could only gawk at her like she had two heads. She wasn't making any sense to him. One, two... what did it mat—

Wait. Willow just said an audience of two... was she trying to tell him... did she mean? His eyes widened in shocked, happy recognition. "Are you? Are we?"

Her eyes sparkled brighter than he'd ever seen them as she bounced on her toes, radiant with excitement. "We're gonna have a baby!"

Practically jumping over the coffee table, he lunged for her and swooped her up in his arms. He twirled her about and kissed her. "We're going to have a baby... oh my God, I'm going to be a dad." The last words came out softly as he gently set her down. He beamed at her happy, ecstatic face.

Without another thought, he sank to the ground, fumbling with pulling the ring from his pocket. "Willow Stevens, before anything else keeps me from asking you what I've been trying to ask you all night..."

He finally pulled the black velvet pouch from his pocket that contained the engagement ring he had made for her. It was one of his errands earlier this afternoon. He shook the ring out of the pouch and onto his palm. "Become my wife. Become my family." Gripping the ring between his thumb and forefinger, he presented her with the round cut diamond on a platinum band adorned with scalloped pave diamonds.

Willow's hand covered her mouth, which he was sure was gaped open in surprise behind her palm. Her watery gaze held his.

"I'm not just asking you to be my wife, to fulfill a prophecy your mother made about us years ago, but because I truly love you. You have my whole heart, not just pieces of it. You taught me that love was more important than duty and I can't imagine living a life without you in it, even when you're mocking and teasing me and calling me a wizard."

At this, they both laughed. Eli sobered before he delivered his next words. "So... will you be my wife? He took her left hand in his and slipped the diamond ring onto her finger.

She was nodding, crying and grinning like a fool before she could actually get out her answer. "Yes. Yes." She admired the ring for a second before falling to her knees and throwing her arms around his neck. The kiss was the best one to date.

Once they broke apart, he rose to his feet and helped pull her up. "Now, I'm ready to finish what you started earlier when I walked in this door."

Willow squealed and ran for the bedroom and he chased her, tackling her to the bed. She rolled onto her back, still giggling. He stared down at her and was leaning in for a kiss when a thought occurred to him. "Do you still have the toga and those gold strappy sandals from Greece?" In his mind he was already seeing her in the sexy outfit.

"Maybe." The coy smile she gave him warmed his blood.

He kissed her softly on the lips. "I want you to wear that during the honeymoon."

"I may be too big with the baby to fit into it." She giggled while she lovingly stroked her still flat belly.

His hand covered hers. "Then I'll just keep you naked on our honeymoon." Even though he was in an amorous mood he still couldn't believe not only would he soon be a husband, her husband, but he'd also be a father. Was it possible to be this happy?

CHAPTER 10

Willow

BLISSFULLY HAPPY DIDN'T begin to describe the way she felt these last few months planning their wedding. They'd finally gotten their normal, a slice of happy and she was eating it up with both hands. Everyone had doted on her and the unborn baby happily baking in her belly. She patted her baby bump.

The last few months had been free of any mishaps; betrayal; intrigue; crazy, vampire, egomaniacs wanting to use her to take over the world or vengeful warlocks. Even when their wedding was announced to the Supernatural world there had been no ugly comments or letters from the zealot group that hated the intermixing of Supernatural factions. The last few months had been a dream.

The only thing that occasionally tainted her sunny disposition during these months was the prophecy, which still loomed like a bad omen. Ever since that night, she'd returned The Book of Prophecy to the cabinet and hadn't touched it since, but the prophecy was etched into her mind. When her mind wasn't preoccupied with wedding plans or baby advice, the niggling thoughts of what the prophecy stated tried to creep in. When that happened she usually busied herself with something or someone.

Many people had come from out of town for the wedding, which would take place tomorrow. Everyone was staying here at Walker house. Hadrian, Lysander, Arsenio and others from the Castellanos coven were in attendance, even the maenads, Nyssa and Damaris had come along. She'd hoped to see a different side of Lysander, but he was still the poster boy for brooding.

It was no surprise that the only members from the Badawi coven were Anippe and Gamal. Their father had sent his best wishes and a wedding gift. She was sure he stayed behind in Cairo to keep the peace and his position as head of the coven.

A large contingent of the Berwick coven from Edinburgh had shown up as well. It was the first time she actually got to talk with Brodie, Hamish or any of the others from their clan as herself since the first time they met she was trapped in Morgana's body. She'd even finally had the chance to meet Ulrik's brother, Rolf who'd come for the wedding as well. Although, Max seemed to think that he came to flirt with Phaedra.

Josephine had been a godsend in helping everything come together. Max was acting as her maid of honor and Phaedra was Eli's best man. Having no family of her own to invite to the nuptials they'd agreed there wouldn't be a groom or bride's side, the guest would all just sit where they wanted.

She was on her way to see Cora. Ever since the Council meted out punishment to Eli for loving her and Cora refused to rescind it, she'd been on the outs with the old woman. The only other time she'd really seen her since then was when Eli talked her into going to ask her about helping find a faery to train her. She still couldn't fathom why she was trudging up the staircase to Cora's chamber. Dragging this extra weight around lately was sometimes a bit taxing, not to mention her bladder was the size of a pea these days. She was just glad the morning sickness had passed.

Finally. She'd made it to the top of the staircase. Knocking once, she entered hoping to catch the nurse inside or Cora out of bed doing something outrageous. When she pushed open the door, she was not the least bit surprised to find Cora in her usual spot: propped against the pillows looking like Bette Davis from *Whatever Happened to Baby Jane?*

Even though she hadn't visited the woman in months, she didn't look the least bit shocked to see Willow enter her bedchamber.

Willow carefully lowered herself to the edge of the bed. Neither said a word for the first few minutes, they just regarded each other.

"Why did you come, child?" Cora croaked out the question, but it wasn't the least bit judgmental or mocking.

"I guess I came... because you were the first one to give me answers about myself. You may not be an Oracle, but I've always felt somehow that you have a sixth sense or the gift of premonition..." Willow rubbed her hand over her bump. "I'm painfully happy, but a feeling keeps creeping in..."

"Willow, you're in Oracle. You'd simply need to ask and more than likely whatever you're wondering about would be shone to you." Again her words were said without malice.

"I know... it's just I'd rather not... I think I'm just being silly. It's only natural when you've had as much happy as I have to expect the other shoe to drop, right?" She gave Cora a smile she didn't quite feel. Part of her wanted to bring up the prophecy, but she decided against it. "Anyways, I came here to bury the hatchet so to speak. With the baby coming and all... I wanted to tell you I'm not angry with you anymore."

Cora placed her hand over Willow's. "I knew that, child."

***

After leaving Cora, she headed back to the apartment. The next morning after Eli found out about the baby, he'd added on an additional bedroom. She woke up and he'd used magic to expand their space. It had been so much fun decorating, painting and putting furniture together the old-fashioned way.

The first time he went to use magic in getting things done, she'd stopped him. She wanted them to spend time together doing everything instead of whipping it together in a matter of seconds. He'd agreed, and there had been times when he was enjoying the preparations even more than she was.

Eli did have his moments of frustration during the assembly of the crib. At one point, he'd begged her to let him use magic, after their third attempt saw the thing falling apart the minute they'd tightened the last screw. She'd finally relented, knowing she couldn't bear the thought of attempting to put it together a fourth time, just to have it fall apart again. At least with it done using magic, she could be sure their poor assembly skills wouldn't result in their baby being injured in a faulty crib accident.

The minute she stepped foot into the apartment, she was greeted with shouts of, "SURPRISE!" In the living room were Max, Zoriana, Anippe, Evie, Josephine and Phaedra.

Max cupped his hands around his mouth and shouted. "Now that the guest of honor is here, let's get this bachelorette party started." Music started playing from somewhere and she smiled, when she thought about him asking Phaedra to help put together a playlist of party music. He kept the music at a respectable level so they could hear each other.

Appetizers were set out and Anippe made her a plate. Evie placed the 'Bride-To-Be' sash over her head and she was helped to a chair that resembled a throne.

Max had taken his duties as maid of honor very seriously she could tell. She laughed when she noticed the bawdy décor of penis balloons, penis straws and other risqué items. It was tough containing her laughter when she caught, Eli's mother sipping from one of the straws. They were taking a break after the second game when she decided to finally ask Zoriana what she'd been wanting to ask her for several weeks, but hadn't quite worked up the nerve.

Willow pulled her aside, into the kitchen. "I wanted to ask you something."

"Okay." She peered at Willow expectantly as she waited.

"Um... I was hoping that since my mother isn't here..." A wistful smile curled her lip. "I was hoping you would give me away."

Tears sprang up in the woman's eyes. Willow knew that since Mathilda was no longer here, Zoriana would never have the opportunity to walk her down the aisle. "I was hoping that this could fill the hole we both carry in our hearts."

"Willow, I would be honored." She embraced her in a hug. When they pulled away, both patted their eyes, clearing away errant tears. "No crying. It's supposed to be a happy day." Zoriana reminded her, even though another tear ran down her cheek.

"Okay."

"Come on you two. We're here to party. As dude of honor, I'm enforcing a fun policy." Max came over throwing feather boas over their shoulders and dragging them back over to the group seated in the living room. Phaedra looked like a hostage wearing the feather boa. Willow tried to stifle laughter when they made eye contact.

"If anyone even thinks of taking a picture of me wearing this... thing... I'll kill you." She picked at the hot pink feather boa like someone had slung a snake around her shoulders instead. When Willow thought about it, she was sure Phaedra probably would have preferred the snake.

Everyone laughed at Phaedra's expense. "C'mon babe, it's not that bad." Max slung his arm over her shoulder and pulled her closer. She leaned in and whispered something in his ear.

"That can be arranged." The heated look that passed between them made Willow blush and turn away. The others had been busy talking and laughing amongst themselves and missed the sexual heat that leapt between the two.

***

"Good night, everyone." At the end of the day, as everyone was leaving the party, she found Hadrian at the door. "Hadrian. It's good to see you." He stepped inside as the last person left.

"I'm so glad you could make it for the wedding." She hugged him.

"I wanted to stop by and spend a brief moment with you before the big day tomorrow."

As he spoke, she walked around picking up stray cups and streamers. "That was very thoughtful of you." She spoke to him over her shoulder as she continued tidying up.

"Let me help you with that." He took the trash bag out of her hand and began picking up the remnants of the party.

For a while they worked in silence.

"When is Eli due back?"

"He's not coming home tonight." She looked over at him and blushed. "We decided to go with the tradition of the groom not seeing the bride the night before the wedding, so he's staying at his parents."

Hadrian tossed more trash into the bag. "You're going to be here alone tonight?" He looked concerned. "Is that wise, I mean with the baby and all?"

"That's so sweet of you, but I won't be alone. Zoriana is coming back tonight and she's going to stay here with me." She really appreciated that Hadrian was acting all fatherly towards her. When she stopped and thought about it, she realized that if her mother was alive, Hadrian could have very well been her stepfather.

Putting down the garbage she was carrying, she grabbed Hadrian's hand and led him to the sofa. "I was just thinking that you must have so many memories running through your head right now of you and my mom... and how different tomorrow might have been if she were still alive."

He nodded and looked at his lap. She hadn't meant to make him sad. She'd done enough wishing her mother would be there tomorrow. Maybe there was a way she could make it special for him too. "I've asked Zoriana to walk me down the aisle tomorrow, but I'd love it if you also walked me down the aisle... kind of as a tribute to my mother, since the two of you were in love." She gave him a hopeful look.

"I would like that very much."

She was about to lean over and hug him when she felt the baby kick. "Oh." She grinned and pressed her hand to her stomach. "The baby has been quite feisty lately." When she looked up, she caught him staring at her stomach strangely. She wondered if he and her mother had talked about having any when they thought they were going to share a life together.

"May I?" He indicated that he was hoping to touch her stomach.

"Yeah." She took his hand and placed it on a spot where she knew the baby would respond. Sure enough, the baby kicked against his hand. He mumbled something incoherent before he looked up at her. "You're right, the baby is quite active. Have you found out the sex?"

"No. We decided we want to be surprised."

Hadrian pulled his hand away and stood up. "I should be going, I'll see you tomorrow." They walked towards the door.

"Tomorrow." She smiled up at him.

Right before he stepped out the door, he turned back to her. "It's a shame your mother couldn't be here to see you."

She could only nod. She felt the same way.

CHAPTER 11

Eli

ANXIOUSNESS WASN'T SOMETHING he expected to feel the day before his wedding, but as he waited for Cosmo, that's exactly what he felt. He was hoping that the faery had been able to find what he asked him to look for since their wedding was happening tomorrow.

He paced the floor in the training room as he waited. Several minutes later, Cosmo arrived.

"So?" He knew he was being rude. He hadn't said hello or even asked Cosmo how he was doing.

Cosmo's smile faltered as he approached. "I'm sorry, Eli. I've had no luck in tracking down Willow's father."

To say he was disappointed would be the understatement of the year. He'd really hoped they could locate him. He'd hoped that Willow would have some family at her wedding.

"If he's still alive, no one knows who he is or they're not coming forward. I put out the details you told me about that night and mentioned Hyacinth, but nothing... Or maybe they don't want to be found. I'm really sorry. I know you wanted to surprise her on her wedding day. Have her father there to walk her down the aisle. You're a good man."

Unfortunately, he wasn't going to deliver on the grandiose gift he'd wanted to gift her with. "Thanks anyway Cosmo. I really appreciate you trying."

"Of course. I would do anything for that girl." Cosmo looked just as disappointed as he did.

"Do me a favor. Just don't tell her we were looking okay? I wouldn't want to get her hopes up or have her disappointed tomorrow." It was no use in both him and Willow being disappointed. He'd known it would be a long shot, but over time, hope had grown. That's what he got for getting his hopes up.

"Our little secret. I'll keep asking around, let you know if anything changes."

"Thanks. See you tomorrow."

After Cosmo left, he decided he should pay his own father a visit. Things had been different between them since Willow's disappearance from Walker house months ago. He wouldn't exactly say that they grew close, but they seemed to have a better understanding of one another. His father had become elated when he heard he would be a grandfather. The look on his father's face when he heard the news surprised him. His impending fatherhood had bonded them.

His father was seated at the dining room table when he arrived. "Where's mom?"

"She's at Willow's bachelorette party." He was flipping through some ledgers when he answered.

"I didn't realize it was that time already. I can only imagine what Max planned." He shook his head and grinned as he took a seat across from his father.

"Mom told you I'll be staying here tonight?"

His father finally looked up from what he was working on. "Yes, she mentioned that the two of you were doing the whole groom not seeing the bride before the wedding thing?"

Eli nodded.

"I thought that kind of tradition was left to couples that weren't already knocked up." For a minute, the look on his father's face was so stern looking. When his face broke into a grin and he laughed, it sounded weird. It was between a snort and a loud guffaw. Given that his father was never one that told jokes before, it could still be a little off-putting when he attempted one.

"Good one dad." It was the only thing he could manage because he wasn't sure if he found it funny or offensive. He'd have to teach his father what constituted a good joke.

"Are you doing a bachelor party?"

"Phaedra's my best man, so whatever she has planned. I kinda hope not. I don't figure Phaedra for the party type, anyway. I can just imagine the barrel of fun she's being at the bachelorette party." This made both of them laugh. He loved his best friend, but he knew shenanigans like whatever Max cooked up would make her unpleasant to be around.

"I'm not getting together with Phaedra until after the bachelorette party... do you want to do something... together? Just you and I?" He had been hesitant to ask the question. Even as a child he couldn't remember the two of them doing too many things together that hadn't included his mother.

His father closed the ledgers and looked at him with a cat that ate the canary sort of look. "That would be nice, but first, there's something I wanted to give you... your wedding present."

"Shouldn't that come after we're married tomorrow?" Eli looked at his father strangely. This was unexpected. He knew for a fact his mother bought any and all gifts that came from the two of them.

"This gift can't wait... and it's actually only for you."

"Okay..." Now he was intrigued. What kind of gift had his father picked out?

When they left his parents home, he admitted he was surprised. He expected his father to lead him to his study and present him with something. When they stood outside the Council Chamber, he was even more puzzled over what the gift could be. There was nowhere to hide anything in that room.

His father pushed the door open and when they walked inside, he found the Elders all seated at the dais. A startled look passed over his face and he gave his father a sharp look. "What's this about?"

He'd never known anything good to come out of being in this room. It had been where he received many a tongue lashing from his father over the way he should handle the Protectors, where he was told he couldn't be with the woman he was about to marry, where he was removed from his command, and the room where he was given the news that he would be stripped of his hereditary magic. Whatever gift his father was going to give him, why did it have to be here? And why were the other Elders needed.

Without answering him, his father left him standing alone and joined the others, taking his seat in the middle of the group.

Eli gulped. The anxiousness he felt earlier, returned.

"Eli Walker..." His father was now all business. "It is with much time, thought and consideration, that The Council of Elders has deliberated and decided to return your hereditary magic back to you."

Eli staggered backwards a few steps in shock. His legs threatened to buckle at the news and he had nothing and no one to hold onto. Did he hear his father correctly? "I don't think I heard you correctly."

His father's face broke into a smile. "We are bestowing the gift of hereditary magic back to you."

He glanced at some of the other members of The Council and found them smiling at him. Disbelief must have still been written on his face, because one of the Elders spoke up. "It's true. You are to have your hereditary magic returned to you this very day."

Another Elder chimed in. "You're the first witch to ever have their hereditary magic returned."

If he was honest, he'd given up hope that they would ever reinstate his hereditary magic. Words failed him. He could only nod and smile with gratitude. Two Council guards materialized next to him and offered to escort him to the stripping room where his hereditary magic would be returned to him. In a daze, he followed behind them, but when he got to the door he paused and turned back to the Elders. "Thank you."

It was meant for all of them, but he locked eyes with his father. His father gave him a subtle nod of acknowledgement before Eli turned and left the room.

As he followed the guards, he held his head high. He puffed out his chest, not with pride, but with conviction. There were so many emotions running through him.

Unlike the last time when he entered the stripping room, he felt no fear or anxiety. The air in the room no longer tasted stale. The sense of loss no longer lingered.

"You've earned this, my boy."

When he looked up into the viewing room, Cora stood there, the same way she had the last time, except this time she was smiling. A short time later, the other Elders joined her.

Once everyone had assembled, she looked to him. Her old frail voice sounding stronger than it should. "Are you ready?"

"Yes." He took his place in the center of the room.

"You'll feel no pain this time. Only elation as the ancestors welcome you home."

As the Elders began chanting, he shut his eyes and allowed himself to be surrounded by the peace and euphoria he felt over once again being connected to his ancestors.

"Maiorum, audierit a senioribus. Ibi unus dignabilis ut habeo tuus daemon et potestatem spirituum. Imbuo illum apud eius hereditatem et quod primogenita vendidisset. Permitto illum audite tuus voces, percipio tuus impes fluit apud eius venas, ita quod autem habet vos apud illum semper."

The words flowed around him and as the spell began to work, he could feel the piece of himself that had been fractured being renewed. His soul was being restored. The rumblings and whisperings of the myriad voices of the ancestors called to his spirit and latched on to it. Their energy fused with his DNA, his very essence and made him whole again.

When the chanting died away and he knew it was over, he opened his eyes. He wanted to leap and shout for joy at being part of the ancestors again. His eyes wandered back up to the viewing room and he saw his father looking down at him. They smiled at one another.

His father met him in the courtyard afterwards. For a minute, he could only stare at his father. No words could convey how thankful he was. He wasn't sure how his father managed to pull it off or talk the rest of the Elders into agreeing, but he was thankful.

He wrapped his arms around his father. "Thank you." He whispered as he tightened his hug. His father embraced him. It was the first time in a long time they had been affectionate with one another. It felt nice to have something better than a hostile relationship with his father, especially with a child on the way.

***

He was on cloud nine as he strolled to Phaedra's apartment for his bachelor party. The minute he'd gotten his hereditary magic back he'd wanted to run to Willow and tell her, but then he remembered his promise that he wouldn't see her until she was walking down the aisle towards him. He hated the idea of telling anyone else before her so as much as it was going to pain him to do so, he wasn't going to say a word to Phaedra.

Willow was going to be his wife. He didn't want to share information with anyone before he shared it with her.

He knocked on Phaedra's door and within seconds she opened the door. Normally, she kept him out here waiting. He was a little surprised to find her alone. There wasn't a streamer, balloon or lewd decoration in sight. He couldn't keep the smile from his face.

She held up an unopened bottle of Lavinia's apple brandy. "Just you, me and the goods stuff."

He stepped inside her apartment.

"I know you didn't want strippers and some big blow out so I just decided to keep it to us... like old times. When you used to whine to me about your daddy issues." She put her hand to her mouth in mock surprise. "Oh wait, that was only a few months ago." While she was laughing he playfully punched her in the arm.

"You always got jokes." He shut the door, came in and dropped onto the floor, leaning back against the sofa. "Open up the brandy."

She joined him on the floor, stretching her legs out underneath the coffee table. "By the way, if I ever decide to get married and it's time for you to plan my bachelorette party you better remember the gift I'm giving you tonight..." She waved her arms around the apartment. "No crazy decorations, sashes you have to wear, or silly games you have to play."

Eli chuckled.

"I promise you, if I see one penis straw or boob top or what have you. It will be your ass." Phaedra finished as she opened up the brandy. "I'm serious." She tried to keep from laughing, but soon she was laughing right along with him.

Once she poured brandy for both of them, she raised her cup in the air to make a toast. "To my best friend on the eve of his wedding..." She cleared her throat. "I wish you and Willow all the happiness in the world. I can't think of someone more deserving than you. Know that I will always have your back, Elias." They knocked their cups together and drank down some of the fiery liquid.

"That was quite the speech. I hope you saved some for tomorrow, when you have to give another toast." He couldn't help teasing her.

"That sappy crap was for your ears only. Tomorrow during my best man speech I'm going to roast you." She guffawed before swallowing a big gulp of the brandy and pouring herself some more.

It had been a while since he'd really heard Phaedra laugh. Of course when they were battling Killian and Morgana, there hadn't been much to laugh about. He hoped that now she would be able to enjoy more days like this.

"Have you thought about finally making an honest man out of Max?" He looked at her over the rim of his cup as he drank. It had been meant partly as a joke, but he was curious how she would answer.

"You know how I feel about marriage."

"That doesn't mean you can't change your mind."

A scowl appeared on her face. She drank down the rest of the brandy in her cup and then refilled it. If it had been anyone else he might have told them to slow down, but he knew Phaedra could hold her liquor.

"I get it..." He sipped at the alcohol and averted his gaze. "If I had someone warming my bed and another someone chasing after me, I might not want to settle down either." He looked away with a smirk on his face.

Phaedra angrily knocked the cup out of his hand.

"Hey." He was thankful he'd drunken most of it. Only a small amount splashed across the carpet. "Don't waste it. It's my bachelor party." He picked up his overturned cup.

"You know I would never cheat on Max." The way she hissed at him, he knew she was pissed.

He held his hands up in surrender. "Whoa. That's not what I meant. I know you wouldn't do that. I was just wondering if there was some other reason you wouldn't want to make things more permanent with Max. You know he loves you."

He was unprepared for her quick retort.

"Everything doesn't have to end in white picket fences and babies, Elias."

He hated that he was responsible for souring the mood. "Listen..." He touched her shoulder. "I'm sorry... I'm being an ass."

Phaedra turned to look at him. There were no traces of amusement on her face.

"I'm being serious. I was being a jerk. You know I just want you to be as happy as I am." They'd been friends for a while, but sometimes he forgot there was much of her past that he knew nothing about. Very little in fact before she came to live at Walker House and be a Walker. She'd never volunteered information and he'd never asked.

"I want us to celebrate my last night as a single man. I didn't mean to ruin it. Let's get shit faced, watch a ton of bad TV and tomorrow during your speech you can roast the hell out of me. Crank the heat all the way up."

This put a genuine smile on her face and she reached for the bottle of brandy. She poured him a new glass and then herself, before she grabbed the remote and turned on the TV.

CHAPTER 12

Willow

SHE COULDN'T STOP twirling in front of the mirror. She had been pleasantly surprised to learn from Josephine shortly after getting engaged that Walker house had its own tailors and seamstresses. It was a husband and wife that had beat the others out to make her dress and they had outdone themselves.

Despite being six months pregnant, with an expanding belly to prove it, they'd designed a gorgeous dress. The floor length gossamer gown had hand-sown appliqué flowers covering the bodice, cap sleeves, waist and in various positions on the skirt. The dress was cut into a deep v-neck and had a low back. Underneath the gossamer was a pale, blush pink, silk slip. She felt absolutely beautiful in the dress. It sucked you only had one wedding day, because she didn't want to ever take this dress off.

A hair stylist styled her curls into a low messy bun. For makeup she'd gone for a natural look, along with a nude lipstick. The only jewelry she wore was some diamond earrings, her snake necklace and the talisman bracelet Eli had given her. All of the finishing touches had been applied. She opted not to have a veil.

Zoriana came up behind her. "You look lovely... your mother would be so proud."

Their eyes met in the mirror. Willow could feel the tears stinging her eyes as she forced them back.

"Don't cry. I don't want you to ruin your makeup. Not before Eli sees you." Zoriana chuckled and pleaded.

Willow took a deep breath and willed the tears to stay where they were. She turned to Zoriana. "I hope it's okay that I asked Hadrian to also walk me down the aisle.

"It's your wedding day. Of course it's fine." She smoothed out the skirt and checked her over once more for any smudges to her makeup or problems with the dress. "Do you have your something borrowed, something blue, something new and something old?" Zoriana ran down the checklist.

"Let's see. I have my something new." Willow lovingly stroked her baby bump and beamed.

"Um, the garter belt I'm wearing is my something blue and my something old..." She touched the snake pendant necklace that she refused to take off on her wedding day, not just because it was the key to The Book of Prophecy, because it was a small piece of her mother. "I guess I don't have my something borrowed." Her forehead wrinkled in frustration. She was sure she had thought of everything, but sometimes pregnancy brain did that to you.

Zoriana unclasped a necklace that had been hidden beneath her dress. When she pulled it out, she saw it was Mathilda's talisman. "Your something borrowed."

Willow was speechless. She had to swallow down the lump that formed in her throat as she turned and let Zoriana put the necklace on her.

"Now you can have a piece of Mathilda with you when you walk down the aisle..." Pausing to collect herself, she brushed back the tears that gathered. "She would have been so excited to see you in your gown and be a bridesmaid." The clasp locked into place and Zoriana adjusted it around her neck. "There you go."

"Remember no tears." She waved her hands in front of Willow's face and then her own, in an attempt to keep either of them from crying.

They both turned to the mirror and stared at the necklace. Their eyes met again in the mirror.

Her eyes assessed her once more and then she smiled. "I think you're ready. Let's get you married."

The square of Walker House had been set up to hold the ceremony. On either side of the makeshift aisle, were chairs covered in blush pink chair covers. The aisle runner was white. The gazebo where they would stand to say their vows was swathed in flowers. The roof portion was covered in hot pink roses.

Cascading down from the roof of the gazebo was fishing line with hot pink roses attached at the top, in the middle blush pink roses and at the bottom white roses, creating an ombre effect. The shower of roses, hung around the outside making it look like the gazebo was enclosed. Each pillar of the gazebo was wrapped in a vine of green leaves and then decorated with roses in the same ombre effect, before ending with a bunch of white roses sitting around the base of each pillar.

When they walked out of the room, everyone stood and turned to look at her as she walked to the top of the aisle where Hadrian waited. Even though she'd performed on stages with people watching her, she felt a small flutter in her stomach as everyone gushed over her and snapped photos. Hadrian took her right arm and Zoriana had her left.

She looked up and found Eli staring at her from the other end of the aisle, underneath the gazebo. Unfortunately, she couldn't keep her promise not to cry. A tear escaped before she could stop it. He looked so handsome in his suit. Her grin widened even further when their eyes met. She was about to walk towards her future.

The music started and she felt like she was gliding during her walk down the aisle. Everyone's eyes were on her, she could feel them, but neither her nor Eli ever took their eyes off of each other. She couldn't help but think how everything in her life had led up to this moment.

At the end of the aisle, Zoriana and Hadrian released her. Eli reached out his hand and she took it, joining him beneath the flower-draped gazebo. It felt like they were the only two in the square and everyone else had disappeared.

The vows seemed to pass by in a blur. She was so love-drunk she was glad all she had to do was repeat her lines, because in this moment she couldn't have remembered what to say on her own.

Once Eli slipped the wedding band onto her finger and the officiant declared them husband and wife, Eli pulled her close and kissed her thoroughly to thunderous applause and catcalls.

They smiled against each other's mouths. After a few more seconds, Eli pulled away, so he could look into her eyes. His lips were still only an inch away from hers. "How does it feel to be Mrs. Willow Walker?" The whispered words were meant for her ears alone.

"Amazing. But, ask me again later, when it's had time to sink in." He grinned and kissed her once more. When they finally broke apart and he took her hand, people were still clapping. They walked down the aisle together with people shouting their congratulations.

A few hours later, wedding photos had been taken, meals served and the dancing was about to get under way. She couldn't remember the last time she'd had so much fun.

Hadrian had agreed to dance with her during a father and daughter dance. Even though he wasn't her father, she appreciated that he would act as a stand in. She did notice that Lysander hadn't seemed too happy about it, but she was not going to let his brooding ruin her big day or her mood. She put her hand in his and let him guide her around the floor to the song.

"Thank you again for doing this. I really appreciate it. You've helped make this day even more special." She hadn't stopped smiling all day.

"You're welcome." He murmured something else, but she didn't catch it.

"What did you say?"

"Nothing at all. Something was caught in my throat.

After their dance ended it was now time for her and Eli's first dance. He joined her out on the floor. When the bump kept Eli from pulling her too close, they both laughed.

"I guess they want daddy to keep his distance right now..." He dropped his voice so only she heard the next words. "You're looking smoking hot in that dress. I can't wait to take it off of you and make love to you all night long." He pressed her as close as he could and swayed with her to the beat of the music.

"Shhh. The baby is going to hear you." She giggled as she teased him.

"The baby's heard worse than that at this point, all the moaning and screaming you do. I didn't know pregnant women could be so horny."

"Eli." Her face flushed and she gave a low squeal while she looked around to see if anyone had heard him. She couldn't help giggling despite trying to be appalled.

He chuckled. "No one heard me... wife." His voice grew husky when he said the word wife.

She felt like she was going to melt into a puddle of desire. "I'm glad... hus..." A sharp pain knifed through her abdomen before she could finish saying the word. Her mouth dropped open at the excruciating pain.

"Willow?" Concern and dread mingled on his face. "What's wrong?"

Perspiration dotted her forehead. "I don't know." She spoke in a hushed whisper while clutching onto him. The next pain was even worse and she gave a strangled gasp and fell against him. She could no longer keep herself upright. "Eli... the baby." It was the last words she got out before she heard ringing in her ears.

It was a matter of seconds before she collapsed. She would have hit the floor, but he caught her.

Eli came into view, as he leaned over her, panicked. He was saying something, but she couldn't hear him, only the ringing. He cupped her face and she tried to focus on him. More people crowded around them. She peered around while she clutched her stomach. *Dear God, please don't take our baby.* Another agonizing pain ripped through her. A scream tore from her throat, but she couldn't hear it. Eli's face contorted in terror and yelling was the last thing she saw before her eyes rolled back into her head and she blacked out.

CHAPTER 13

Eli

"GIVE US SOME room!" He shouted as he attempted to exit the reception carrying his unconscious wife. So many people had gathered around to help and now he was having trouble getting out of the throng.

One minute they were dancing, flirting and joking and the next she was in pain and screaming. His heart was in his throat. Was it the baby? Were they about to lose their unborn child?

"Out of the way!" He bellowed once more and that seemed to part the crowd like the Red Sea. He hustled her out of the room and being out of the crowd allowed him to think more clearly and he teleported them into their apartment.

Quickly, he laid her on the bed. He could already hear pounding on the door. He was sure Phaedra, Max and

Zoriana had teleported to the apartment, but they couldn't have teleported inside since it wasn't their living space. He tuned it out for the time being.

He rubbed her cheeks. *What happened?* At least he could no longer see the horror stricken look on her face she'd had before she blacked out. That would forever be burned into his memory.

His hands began to feel along her body, looking for an injury or wound. There was nothing, not even any blood.

"Willow?" He called to her, willing the sound of her name to wake her up. Nothing.

The pounding on the door had gotten louder. Since he couldn't find anything wrong and she hadn't woken, he figured she would be fine for a few seconds while he opened the door. He was sure they were worried about her.

They all came spilling into the apartment the minute he opened the door: Zoriana, Max, Phaedra, his parents, Alistair, Hadrian, Lysander, Evie and Delaney.

"How is she?" His mother asked immediately.

"She's still unconscious." His voice was vacant and hollow when he answered her.

"What happened?" Phaedra was already in Protector mode.

"What can we do?" Zoriana asked.

"Son, do you need anything?" His father looked at him with concern.

"How's the baby?" Either Delaney or Evie asked, but at this point all of their questions had blended together becoming a cacophony of noise he could not decipher.

He stepped away from them. "Just give me a minute." He mumbled trying to retreat. All of their questions were just too much. He winced.

"Should we send for a doctor?"

"Cora was asking for an update. What should I tell her?"

"What should we tell the guests?"

"You don't look so well."

"Maybe you should have a seat. I'll get you a glass of water."

"Should someone go in and sit with Willow?"

It was all too much. He had no idea who was asking what. He clapped his hands over his ears and squeezed his eyes shut in angry frustration. "Shut up!"

Immediately, everyone stopped. Slowly, he opened his eyes and dropped his hands to his sides.

This wasn't how this day was supposed to go. He walked into the kitchen to escape everyone and be alone. He braced his hands on the countertop and exhaled.

He hung his head. They'd just gotten married. They were finally getting their happy after Killian and Morgana and the whole fiasco with her possibly being dead. Three months, that's how long it had taken for trouble and misfortune to find them again.

I can't lose either of them.

"What do you need?" Phaedra's strong voice was at his back. "I've sent everyone away. Zoriana is in the bedroom, sitting with Willow and Max is in the living room waiting for instructions. Just tell me what you need."

He was so grateful for her strength and leadership right now, because he couldn't think straight, let alone make a decision. All he could think about was their unborn child. The way Willow clutched her stomach and doubled over made him believe the problem had been with the baby. For over a minute, he didn't respond.

"She can't lose the baby..." Without turning to look at her, he finally spoke the words he was afraid of. "If she wakes up and I have to tell her we lost the baby, I don't think she'll recover... Hell, I don't know if I'll recover." He ran his hand through his hair. He was trying his best to keep it together.

"We don't know anything yet." She came up beside him and put her hand on his shoulder. "Why don't we get the doctor here and let them assess her?"

He nodded his consent while he unknotted his tie and pulled it from around his neck. It had begun to feel like a noose tightening around his throat. He breathed a little easier once it was off. Phaedra guided him back to the sofa and stepped away to place the call. Max brought him a glass of water while they waited.

Once the doctor arrived they all crowded into the bedroom, none of them wanting to be left out. He knew how important Willow was to each of them as well and he didn't make them leave. Having them there brought him a measure of comfort. After the examination, the doctor declared that she could find nothing wrong physically and reassured them all that the baby was okay. She couldn't tell them when Willow would wake up, just that they had to be patient.

Last time Willow was unconscious it lasted a month. He knew this time her unconscious state wasn't due to her soul being outside her body, but he still worried. All they could do was wait. He sent everyone home shortly after the doctor left. Pulling up a chair to the bedside, he prepared to wait, as long as it took her to wake up.

CHAPTER 14

Willow

WHEN HER EYES opened she was staring at the ceiling. At first she felt disoriented. The last thing she remembered was dancing with Eli. She leaned up on her elbows and found she was lying in their bed, still wearing her wedding dress. Someone had removed her high heels.

When she looked around she found Eli asleep in a chair next to the bed. His appearance looked haggard. His tuxedo jacket and tie had been abandoned and his shirtsleeves were rolled up to his elbows.

Memories of the excruciating pain flooded her brain and then she recalled collapsing. Instinctively, her hand went to her belly. She rubbed her bump and felt a tiny kick. The relief that their baby was safe was so overwhelming as it washed over her that she nearly broke down crying. Some wanted to blame all of her erratic emotions on pregnancy hormones, but she knew that wasn't the case. Just like she knew that something was definitely wrong with their baby.

"You're awake."

Before she could even say anything, she was in his arms. "Are you okay? Do you need anything? The doctor said everything looked fine." His eyes were filled with worry despite what he'd told her the doctor said.

"I feel fine."

"What happened? What do you think caused it?"

She tried to think back to right before it happened. "I honestly don't know." There was no way she would tell him of her fear. There was no sense in both of them being scared yet, if there wasn't anything to be worried about.

Hopefully, the smile she plastered onto her face seemed genuine. "I'm okay. The baby's okay." She was doing her best to alleviate any fear he had. She smoothed his hair down that stuck up at odd ends probably from where he'd been running his fingers through it all day in frustration. "Why don't we just go to bed?"

He didn't resist. They both undressed and got under the covers. He spooned her from behind, keeping one hand on their baby all night. While he fell asleep instantly, she lay there most of the night with her unsettling thoughts, running through her mind.

***

The next morning she was up early despite her troubled sleep. She showered quickly and closed the bedroom door on a sleeping Eli. After what he'd been through yesterday, she was sure he could use the rest.

She went to the cabinet where she'd locked away The Book of Prophecy and pulled it out. When she set it on the coffee table, a cloud of dust wafted up into the air. She blew some of it off the cover and stared at the book. A short time later after deliberating, she removed the snake necklace and watched as the pendant changed into the shape of a key when it neared the keyhole.

The book sat unopened for long minutes before she could bring herself to turn the pages. It was like the book had a mind of its own, like it knew what she was searching for, because in the next second, it landed on the page with the prophecy she read months ago. She didn't let herself think about what that could mean. Gently, she picked the tome up off the coffee table and settled it on her lap. She read the prophecy again.

Rekehwer 602 BC

Temple of Amun

(village of Aghurmi in Siwa Oasis)

Egypt

Oracle: Amenirdis

While the Sibyls meditate and await my instructions I wanted to put down the troubling vision I had today.

I'm not sure how far into the future it will happen, but it was revealed to me that a future Oracle will birth a child that could contain a powerful, unspeakable evil that will further spread hatred and division or a force used for good, to heal and unite factions that had once been violently divided. The vision has been shown to me several times and each time there is no definitive conclusion. One thing that is shown is that the Oracle may have to sacrifice this child for the sake of mankind.

The entry raised so many historical questions that she couldn't even begin to dive into right now. As much as she tried to shy away from it, she had to figure out if this prophecy was about their unborn child or she would never have peace.

There was more that had been troubling her since she woke up this morning. Given her due date, she'd been able to determine that she'd conceived the day they took that bath together, which meant, she was pregnant when her spirit left her body. Cosmo had told her that her soul could commune with the dead. What if some malevolent spirit had hitched a ride before she got back to her body?

She looked at the prophecy again. It stated that an evil would be contained in the child. If this prophecy spoke of their baby... and she really hoped that was a big if. That evil would not have come from her or Eli. This child knew how much it was loved. The only reasonable explanation would be an outside force that sought to control their child, which when she thought about it, their child would end up being quite powerful in their own right, considering they would be the Oracle, part fae and have Eli's hereditary magic.

Shutting the book, she struggled to get up from the sofa. Once she did, she put the book away and headed to the library. She needed answers. Along the way, she called Cosmo to meet her. What she couldn't find in books, she knew he would be able to answer right away.

***

She'd been searching books for over an hour before Cosmo turned up. It was hard not to be irritated he hadn't come sooner, but she realized she hadn't told him it was an emergency. She pushed the book away that Enid had found for her when she came in.

"I'm so glad to see you're well. I was concerned when you collapsed at your wedding." Cosmo sat across from her.

For a brief moment, she wondered about his age again. He was always coy when she asked him. She dropped that line of thought instantly. Right now it wasn't important.

"Thank you. I'm fine." She scooted closer to the table and dropped her voice. She was sure they were the only ones in the library, but she was sure Enid eavesdropped and didn't want to be overheard. "I need to ask you some questions about possession."

His discerning eyes bore into her. "What exactly is it that you want to know?"

Her throat was dry. She swallowed before she began. "I was outside of my body for a long time. Plus, I lost the tether that you mentioned, which is why I think it took me so long to get back. Was my body just stuck in some sort of limbo during that time?"

He shook his head. "Remember I told you that while your soul is out of your body it's in the realm of the dead until you return back to your body." He was only feeding her bits and pieces she could tell. He seemed to be waiting for her to just come out and ask what she wanted to know.

"Does that mean that other souls or spirits can communicate with me? Dead souls?"

Seconds ticked by while he stared at her. "You know this already."

"Would a soul try to come back from the dead by attaching itself to you?" She leaned her elbows on the table and waited for an answer.

"Not necessarily... most souls that are dead have made their peace and found contentment in the afterlife. They know the consequences of trying to come back, especially as part of another soul or trying to take over a soul before their time..." He now leaned forward onto the table as well.

"However, if the host body you were recently inhabiting died or was on the verge of death before you left and their soul or spirit was strong enough and had a good reason for wanting to stick around, they might be desperate enough to chance it, by attaching part of their soul to you to escape death."

A chill ran up her spine and her blood ran cold. All over she broke out in a cold sweat. She'd never considered the possibility of that happening. It couldn't be.

"Willow? Are you okay?" Cosmo touched her hand and she recoiled. He pulled his hand away from her and sat back in his seat.

"Sorry... sorry... it's not you. I just..."

"What are you not saying? You've been holding

something back this entire time, with this whole line of questioning to things you already know the answer to... let me help you." He edged forward again, but did not attempt to touch her.

She needed to tell someone. She couldn't keep this to herself anymore. Maybe, he could help her. With a trembling, shaky breath she looked down at the table and spoke. "As she was dying, we struggled and fought while I was trying to leave her body. She was trying to keep me there so I would die with her. I narrowly escaped before she took her last breath..." Finally, she looked at Cosmo. "I think before she drew her last breath, Morgana attached a piece of herself to my unborn child and now she wants to control or possess it." A tear slid down her face. She omitted the part about the prophecy.

CHAPTER 15

Eli

ELI JUST NEEDED to keep busy. Even though there was no longer the threat of Killian or Morgana, it didn't mean there still wouldn't be a new threat at some point or those evil bastards of the Supernaturals Against Hybrids hate group wouldn't show up and decid to cause trouble. So, the Protectors needed to train and stay in tip top shape.

The only one who was excused was Willow. He hadn't shared with anyone that he was worried about her. Over the last week, she tossed, turned and whimpered in her sleep at night. He wasn't sure if she was having nightmares. Smudges were under her eyes from lack of sleep and where she once had a healthy pregnant glow, she often seemed listless. She hadn't said anything to him yet, but he could tell she was keeping something from him. He hoped if he gave her time and space, she would confide in him.

There hadn't been any episodes like what happened at the wedding and for that he was thankful. Everyone checked on her regularly, which he appreciated.

After a long day of training, he walked in to find her sitting on the sofa, staring at the TV with a vacant look in her eyes.

"Hey babe." He infused his voice with tenderness as he sat next to her on the couch and pulled her into his side. He dropped a kiss on the top of her head. It took a second for her to relax into him. When she finally did it felt like she was unloading some invisible burden.

He stroked her arm and wished she would tell him whatever was plaguing her, because it was sucking the life out of her.

"Hey baby." She finally said in a far off voice like she was deep in thought.

Suddenly, it occurred to him that he'd never gotten to share his good news with her like he'd intended on their wedding day. All the fear and worrying seemed to take center stage since the incident and his good news had gotten buried in the back of his mind.

He sat up and turned to her. His movements caused her to look up at him.

"On our wedding day I meant to share some news with you and then the incident happened and I forgot."

She sat up a little straighter. "What is it?"

"As a wedding gift, my dad and the Elders restored by hereditary magic."

The news seemed to have the desired effect on her that he was hoping for. Her eyes lit up with excitement and she threw her arms around him. "Seriously? How could you forget that kind of news? That's wonderful. Does anyone else know?"

"You're the first person I wanted to tell. You and the little munchkin here." He looked down and rubbed her belly.

She scooted away from him and tried to stand on her own. The hurt lasted for only a second. *Was she pulling away from me? Maybe I imagined it.* He got up and helped her stand. She accepted his help, so he reassured himself what he perceived a minute ago wasn't the case.

"We should celebrate with everyone, Phaedra, Max, Zoriana, Edie, Delaney, your parents." She rambled on as she waddled to the bedroom. He followed her.

"Everyone should know about your news. I'm sorry I messed everything up and we didn't celebrate sooner."

He turned her around to face him. "You have nothing to apologize for." He bent and kissed her. She pressed herself against him. Again, it was confirmation that he'd gotten it wrong earlier. She hadn't pulled away from him. He smiled into her mouth.

When they pulled apart, she continued with plans. "I'll call your mother and see if she's up for hosting a dinner party. I just don't have the energy."

An hour later they were all seated around his parents table. His mother had been too happy to host. Everyone congratulated him over getting his hereditary magic returned.

Willow's mood had improved considerably. She chattered away with everyone during the meal. He was so glad to see her back to her old self. Maybe this was exactly what she needed. He was content to just watch her. Her rounded belly had him thinking about the sex of their unborn child. They hadn't really started throwing names around yet, they'd been so preoccupied with the wedding the last few months. Plus, since they decided to wait to know the sex of the baby, it hadn't prompted them to start choosing names. He knew they said they would wait, but he started wondering if he could get her to change her mind. He was anxious to know if they were having a Mikaela, or a Dylan, a Tristan or a Kendall. *Maybe a Camilla?* Lost in his daydream of baby names he slid his hand over the bump.

The moment he touched her stomach, she flinched and jerked backward slightly. Their eyes locked and he did his best not to let the shocked hurt show, but it was too late. He saw in her eyes that she knew she'd wounded him. She opened her mouth to say something, but closed it again.

Thankfully, no one else saw the moment that passed between them. He hadn't been wrong earlier. Did she not want him? Did she not want the baby? He didn't know what to think.

The food tasted like ash in his mouth the rest of dinner. Conversation went on around him, but he sat there like a stunned bird, only giving monosyllable answers whenever someone asked him a question. Willow allowed herself to be pulled into conversation, but often she would glance warily in his direction.

They weren't even a month into their marriage and already something was wrong.

When dinner ended, the walk back to the apartment was agonizing, with each turn down another hallway that drew them closer to home, he dreaded each step.

He unlocked the door and let her step inside. Walking into the kitchen, he grabbed some water from the fridge and stood in there guzzling it. Avoidance. He was looking for any reason, any excuse not to go back out into the living room and have the conversation about why she didn't want him touching her.

Nearly thirty minutes later, he'd scrubbed every already clean service, washed the few dishes in the sink, put the dishes in the dishwasher away, drunk another bottle of water, swept the floor, and thrown out some leftovers from a couple of days ago. He had nothing left to do. It was time to face the music.

Unfortunately, when he came out Willow had already gone to bed. He didn't have the heart to wake her so he just lay down beside her and instead of curling himself around her like he normally would have done; he kept to his side of the bed.

CHAPTER 16

Willow

THE YOUNG GIRL was a mixture of the two of them. She had her curls, nose and cheekbones and Eli's eyes, chin and smile. She was beautiful. Unfortunately, her soul was tainted by Morgana's possession of her. The evil gleam Willow saw in her eyes as she killed and destroyed in her quest to rule was frightening.

Their daughter now stood outside Walker house. She raised her hand and shattered the door with magic before stepping through. Willow only heard the sounds of the slaughter: witches trying to fight back; tortured screams before death claimed her victims. She was a young girl, but thanks to Morgana, she already had an army of warlocks ready to do her bidding. The threat of Killian paled in comparison to what would come with Morgana exacting her revenge and getting exactly what she'd hoped for. After killing all of Walker house, she located what she came for, her mother's Grimoire. With the ancient book of black magic and all the extra powers of being the Oracle and part fae, she would be unstoppable. She could now set out to bend everyone to her will. Serve her or die.

"No! No! I won't let you have her." She sobbed and screamed. Lashing out at some unseen force she was unaware that Eli was now bearing the brunt of her slaps, punches and kicks until he finally shook her awake.

"Willow! Wake up!"

Her eyes popped open and she stopped her assault. She was in her bed. It was just a vision. Unfortunately, she couldn't take solace in the fact that it was just a vision. It was a vision that would more than likely come true.

Eli sat back against the headboard. "We should talk."

She knew this was coming. Last night, she'd gone to bed the minute they arrived home in an attempt to escape "talking" last night, but now she was going to have to tell him. She'd seen the hurt in his eyes at dinner and felt guilty for making him think it was anything he'd done. She had hoped to spare him this knowledge, but she knew she couldn't any longer.

She was expecting his anger, but when he looked at her, all she saw was hurt and dread.

"Have I done something wrong? Do you regret marrying me? I knew something was wrong before yesterday, I just hadn't realized I was the problem before yesterday, when twice you wouldn't let me touch you."

She hated hearing the uncertainty in his voice.

'It wasn't me I didn't want you to touch." The minute she said it, she realized how awful it sounded and that he wouldn't understand. She didn't want him falling in love with the child, knowing it could grow up to be a monster.

That comment made him look even more wounded than he already was. "You don't want me to touch my own kid?"

How could she begin to tell him? "No, it's not like that."

He took her hand in his. "Just tell me."

"We're going to have a daughter... I've seen her." The words weren't said with any pleasure; they scraped her throat coming out. Tears trickled down her face.

A smile lit up his face from the inside out and she hated that her next words were going to kill his joy and rob him of the excitement of learning the sex of his child. "Why are you crying? That's wonderful news." With the pads of his thumbs he wiped away her tears. He was love drunk on baby news.

"At dinner, I was starting to think about names. Now that we know it's a girl. What about Camilla?"

This made her cry harder. Eli pulled her into his lap despite her struggles. "Stop." Calmly, he tried to soothe her. When his eyes gazed into hers, she finally stopped resisting him. He placed his hand firmly on her stomach and massaged her belly. "We're going to have a little girl." He crooned. "I hope she looks exactly like you." He kissed the side of her head.

"I have to tell you something and you have to promise to let me finish the whole story before you say anything."

He was about to protest.

"Promise me." Her eyes pleaded with him to understand.

He nodded.

"While my soul was outside my body I was in the realm of the dead. Cosmo told me when he taught me about possession that I would be able to communicate with the dead..." Her eyes stayed glued to his face as she told the story. "What I didn't know was that, if a dead soul wants out bad enough they will sometimes latch onto you to escape death." She could see her words were beginning to sink in.

Unshed tears clogged her throat. She cleared it before she continued speaking. "I thought it may have been a random spirit that latched onto me... but a week ago, Cosmo told me that when you're leaving a host body that's dying... if that soul is strong enough it can latch onto you..."

He shut his eyes and pinched the bridge of his nose, like he was willing what she said not to be so.

Willow sniffled and scrubbed the back of her hand across her nose. "Morgana fought tooth and nail to keep me in her body, trying to kill me when she died. I got out right before she died and I think she latched onto..."

Eli interrupted her. "You think she latched onto you?"

She shook her head. "Not just me... I think she latched onto the baby."

"What?" The misery and heartache in his voice was so wretched, it was too much, but she had to continue. She swiped the tears away.

"The reason I'm sure is because the day after I came back, I opened up The Book of Prophecy and read from it. In there was a prophecy about an Oracle birthing a child that would be an unspeakable evil and she would have to make a choice to kill it to save the world."

"No." He wailed.

"Based on the prophecy, there is a good chance that she will be evil and destroy the world, especially if it's as I suspect and Morgana has latched onto her..." Her voice was becoming shrill now. "I didn't want you to touch my belly and bond with her, like I already had, knowing... I, we... may have to kill her to keep her from becoming some abomination that Morgana will turn her into." She sobbed in his arms after getting it all out.

He stared at her aghast. What she saw written on his face went beyond shock. It was probably closer to revulsion.

"Kill our own kid?" The sound that came out of him was so broken. "Are you sure, the prophecy is about our baby?" His eyes were red-rimmed and glassy from fighting back his own tears. He was grasping at straws. They both knew it. She felt awful when the realization settled on his face. "There has to be another way." He pulled her tighter and just held her.

CHAPTER 17

Eli

NEITHER OF THEM slept the rest of the night. They'd gotten up at some point so he could read the prophecy for himself. Afterward, they went back to the their bed and just lay together, holding one another, with their unborn daughter nestled between them.

Eli felt guilt over Willow dealing with that all alone. He should have asked her sooner what was wrong. Right now they needed to figure out how to deal with this, but also get confirmation that a piece of Morgana's soul had in fact latched onto Willow and their baby.

It was barely six o'clock in the morning. The only thing he could think to do was to involve the Elders. This had to be put to them so a decision could be made on what to do. Maybe Morgana could be removed. There had to be some spell that would fix this, despite what the prophecy said.

They held hands. They hadn't let go of one another since she told him everything. This was his family and he wasn't going to give up any part of it without a fight. That bitch Morgana had another thing coming if she thought she was going to take his baby girl.

"Get up baby." He sat up. "I'm going to call everyone together and ask them to meet us in the Council's chamber."

When she sat up, he cupped her face in his hands. Her face was tear streaked and her eyes were red and puffy, but to him she was still beautiful. "I need you to be the fighter I know you are. That bitch isn't taking our girl."

She nodded and looked back at him with a strong, steady gaze despite her bottom lip quivering for just a moment. "Okay."

***

Many of the Elders filed into the room stifling yawns and shrugging on their robes to cover the pajamas they still wore. Shortly after he and Willow arrived, Phaedra and Max showed up with Evie and Delaney close on their heels.

"As soon as I got the message we came. Is everything okay?" Phaedra looked between him and Willow.

Willow sniffled. She wouldn't pick her eyes up from the floor.

Max sensed something was off and moved closer to Willow. He whimpered. "Willow? What's wrong?"

Eli knew this was hard. It was hard on them both. "Max, please let everyone get here and then I promise we'll tell everyone."

Max nodded, but his concern for Willow didn't lessen. He scooted closer and rubbed her back. His whimpering didn't stop either.

Zoriana showed up with Alistair trailing her. "We got here as soon as we could."

His mother and father were the last to arrive and then Archie closed the door to the chamber. After his father took his seat on the dais with the other Elders he gave Eli his undivided attention. "You called this meeting. The Council yields the floor to you."

Eli put his arm around Willow and together they walked forward. "It concerns our child."

No one spoke.

He looked around at all the anxious faces and decided the best course of action was to say it plainly. "When Willow escaped her possession of Morgana's body, before she was killed... we believe a piece of her soul attached itself to the baby... our daughter."

What should have been a joyous occasion followed by oohing and aahing was instead marked by shocked gasps.

Josephine rushed over and grabbed Willow's hand. She was already teary eyed over hearing the news. "Are you sure?"

One of the Elders spoke up. "Can't we just exorcise Morgana's spirit from Willow's body?"

People began to talk over one another, trying to be heard.

"There's more." Eli's raised voice silenced everyone. "In the Book of Prophecy, there is a prophecy that tells of an Oracle that will give birth to a child that possesses great power that quite possibly contains an unspeakable evil that will devastate this world... or her powers could be used to heal it. The outcome of the vision was unclear, but the prophecy stated that it was a good possibility that the oracle would have to kill her child to save mankind."

The room would have erupted into chatter once more, but Eli raised his hand for silence. "I believe that Morgana's evil, vengeful spirit wants to be reborn as my child so she could wreak havoc on the world, which is why I believe that Willow is the Oracle that is spoken of in the prophecy... we need your help to save her."

At this, the noise level in the room increased. People swarmed the two of them, trying to offer comfort, solace and reassurance.

His father called for order. Emotions warred on his face, while he tried to exude leadership and take charge of the situation, it was clear the father and grandfather in him was greatly distraught over this news. It was his grandchild after all that would end up being the casualty if this prophecy came true. Everyone quieted down so he could speak. "First, we must be sure that Morgana has in fact attached her spirit to the unborn child... we will need Cora for the ritual."

Guards were sent to bring Cora to the chamber. The rest of them prepared the room for the ritual that would need to be performed to determine if Morgana was in fact trying to possess their daughter.

Phaedra and an Elder witch began drawing a pentacle on the floor of the Council chamber. Zoriana, Delaney and Alistair were sent to fetch the crystals that were needed.

"Listen to me." He placed his hands on Willow's shoulders and looked into her eyes. "When Cora arrives she is going to be the one to run the ritual. You have to be part of it."

Willow clutched his arm, frightened by what she was being asked to do. He could see she was tired. Her bloodshot eyes skittered away from his to look at the symbol being marked on the floor. "What am I going to have to do?" She watched as they began to set up the crystals around the pentacle. Her body trembled against him.

"I'm going to be right here. I won't let anything happen to you." He soothed her, trying to banish her fear.

As he held her, he watched Zoriana and some of the others set up the fluorite, black obsidian, staurolyte and spirit quartz crystals around the pentacle. The crystals were supposed to help in the protection of both Cora and Willow, during the ritual. When he saw people's heads turning to look at the door, he turned too. Guards flanked Cora on either side as she walked into the room. He knew the old woman was frail, but she must have insisted on walking down here on her own two feet. Her eyes found them and stayed locked on them as she approached.

"I'm sorry my child."

Willow let the old woman embrace her. Cora stepped back to look at her and then her swollen belly. She placed her hands on Willow's stomach. Cora took Willow's hand as the preparations were completed. She led her towards the pentacle, but Willow would not let go of his hand.

"It's okay." He reassured her and placed a kiss upon her forehead.

She let go of his hand and allowed Cora to lead her to the middle of the pentacle. Zoriana and Evie stepped in and helped Willow lay on the ground and then stepped out again.

Cora walked around the edge of the pentacle in a circle chanting protection spells. The woman's body might have appeared frail, but he could tell that she was much stronger than one would think. Nervously, Willow raised her head to watch. It was very clear when the actual ritual got under way because Cora lifted her arms upwards and shouted loudly. "Mali spiritus, consurgetis de insidiis et ipsum relevare."

The room went still and quiet as she repeated the incantation once more. On the third recitation, the candles in the room flickered and then Morgana's spectre appeared in the pentacle with Cora and Willow. There was a collective intake of breath when everyone saw her materialize. She looked similar to what she looked like before her death: pale and covered in blood, despite that, she was grinning.

"What is it that you seek?" Cora asked her in a no-nonsense tone.

Eli looked at Willow to see how she was doing. He could see the shallow breaths she was taking, because she was terrified. One hand was clutched over her baby bump.

Morgana walked around the pentacle. "You know what I want." The smile that had been on her face was gone in an instant, replaced by eyes filled with wrath and an evil sneer on her lips. "You let me be raised in this house, in this coven, under a lie and you think I won't make all of you pay?" She looked around the room at her audience. "I want what you denied my mother. When I'm human again. I'll raise her up."

"You know we will stop you." Cora admonished her, never once changing tone or showing emotion to anything she'd said so far.

"Death hasn't stopped me. Even now I'm powerful. I have the magic of the ancestors, plus my mother's ancient black magic at my back... and this child..." Her spirit leaned over a squirming Willow. She reached out a hand to caress her belly. "This child is going to help me grow stronger and mightier."

"Siphoner magic." His father mumbled at his side. Eli looked at him before returning his gaze back to the circle.

"Leave her be." Cora's voice snapped at her in an authoritative tone that brooked no disobedience.

Morgana stepped away from Willow and smiled a nasty smile again. "I'm already in her belly, Cora. The baby's mine and you can't stop it." The words were so sinister.

Eli wanted to rush in, use his magic, do anything, but he knew if he broke the circle that had been set up it could be perilous to not only Cora, but to Willow as well.

Morgana stepped toward Willow again.

"I said leave her be." The forceful words came out of Cora, followed by her raising her hand and blasting Morgana with a bolt of white energy. It knocked Morgana away, and for a minute she appeared hurt, but then she countered Cora's magic, by blasting her with a powerful bolt of black energy that lifted Cora off her feet, launched her in the air and caused her to land on her back outside the circle.

Morgana dove into Willow's body. Willow cried out as she writhed on the ground in agony. Morgana was doing who knew what to her and the baby.

"Do something." He yelled at the witches that were standing around.

"Eli." Willow shrieked, as her body was wracked by more pain.

Cora clambered back to her feet and said some words he could not hear over Willow's tortured screams. Everything went still again, even Willow's screams stopped. Her body spasmed once more and then went limp.

Whatever she said seemed to make it safe to enter the pentacle because everyone moved at once. He raced towards Willow, but looked at Cora with concern. She'd taken a nasty fall when Morgana knocked her out of the circle. Some of the Elders, along with Delaney and Evie were helping her to a chair.

Willow was unconscious when he reached her. Wisps of hair were plastered to her forehead. She was sweating all over and seemed to have a fever. He picked her up in his arms. She seemed so small. A lump was in his throat. Her body had endured so much and still she was holding on.

"Eli." The old woman's croak turned his head. She was standing and being supported by one of the Elders. "You have my word that we will do everything in our power to save them both."

He turned with Willow in his arms and headed for the door. After she told him everything last night, he'd raged against the idea of losing his child. Not once until just now upon hearing Cora's words had he ever thought he could lose not only his child, but Willow too. That was not something he was prepared to accept.

CHAPTER 18

Willow

FOOD WOULD NOT stay down. Every time she ate, she would vomit. She hadn't left the bed in the last three days, not since the ritual that determined Morgana was in fact haunting her belly. At different times throughout the day her body would experience horrible pains courtesy of Morgana.

Phaedra, Max and Zoriana were helping Eli, by sitting with her in shifts. Recently, Max had tried to get her to eat some bone broth the kitchen had prepared for her, but she refused. The last thing she wanted was to puke in the bucket that now lived next to her bed.

Max now lay at the foot of the bed in dog form. In the past, this always made her feel better. It bought her some measure of mental comfort, but her body was in physical pain. Between the stomachaches from not eating and constant vomiting, she had to deal with the agonizing pains of Morgana's torture. Her head ached from screaming when the violent pains ripped through her, which caused her throat to be raw.

Huddling beneath the blanket Max covered her with earlier when she refused the broth, she shivered.

The front door opened. Max raised his head up off his paw and sniffed the air. When he was satisfied he knew who entered he lay his head back down. Eli's heavy footfalls carried through the living room until he reached the bedroom. She didn't need to turn over to know he was standing in the doorway.

Seconds ticked by before his deep voice filled the silence. "Max, I want to be alone with my wife."

Max, whined once, but jumped off the bed and went into the living room. Eli shut the door behind him. The bed dipped and then his arms were around her.

"Lysander and Hadrian have returned from Greece to help." Eli was doing his best to make her feel better.

She didn't say anything.

"You didn't eat your broth."

"It wouldn't have stayed down anyway." She was glad he was here, but she didn't want him fussing over her.

"Baby..." He said the endearment softly while he nuzzled her neck. "You have to eat for the baby. You have to try." The last sentence came out as a plea.

A tear slid down her cheek. She swiped it away. "Eli..." Her throat was so hoarse that his name came out on a croak. She cleared her throat. "I want to eat... I want to nourish the baby. I do..." She let out a breath. "But I don't want her..." She put the emphasis on her. "To grow stronger. I don't." More tears fell and this time she didn't bother to wipe them away.

Eli turned her onto her back. His voice was gentle. "You know that's not the way this works." His eyes reflected a tenderness, which she didn't feel she deserved. "Morgana is a spirit. She isn't effected by you starving yourself, but our daughter is. I need you to try to eat. Please." His fingers caressed her cheek.

She didn't want him to think she didn't care about the baby. "You know I love her." She placed her hands over her stomach and lovingly caressed the bump.

"I know."

After being alone for most of her life after her mother died, she finally had a family of her own. Unfortunately, life was hell bent on taking that from her. "Why is this happening?" She quietly sobbed, while clutching his shirt. Normally, she hid her tears or tried to stifle them, but she was so tired.

"We're going to get through this." He leaned over and kissed her forehead.

She willed herself to stop crying. She used the backs of her hands to wipe away the tears. Eli and their daughter needed her to be strong and that's what she was going to do, get herself strong so she could fight this bitch. It was a struggle because she was malnourished, but she pushed herself up to sit against the headboard. "Give me the broth."

The warm smile that Eli gave her warmed her insides. He leaned up on his elbow and reached across her to the nightstand where the bowl sat. He grabbed the spoon.

"I don't need you to feed me. I can do it myself."

He shrugged and placed the bowl in her hands. She hadn't meant the words to come out so harshly. She was just tired of people waiting on her.

"I'm sorry. I just... I miss my independence. I'm not used to not doing for myself... It makes me feel helpless." After her apology and confession she turned to look at him. There was no trace of anger anywhere on his face.

"I know." He rubbed his hand up and down her arm. "Eat." He nodded toward the bowl.

She gave him a weak smile before turning her attention back to the bowl. She lifted it to her mouth and drank some. Then she waited a beat before drinking anymore, trying to see if her stomach would reject it. When she didn't instantly start retching she drank some more. She could feel his eyes on her. "Stop watching me eat... I look like a hot mess." She sipped at the now tepid broth.

"No, you don't. You look beautiful." He leaned over with a grin and kissed her cheek.

"You're just saying that, because you don't want me to know how hideous I really look."

"No, it's the truth. I think you look beautiful." When she looked in his eyes she could tell he really meant it.

Fifteen minutes later, she was finishing the last of the broth when someone knocked on the bedroom door.

"Come in." Eli called out, but didn't get up from the bed.

Max, now back in human form and wearing his usual California surfer attire, poked his head in. "You guys have a visitor. Hadrian's here, he said he just wanted to check on Willow."

She smiled. "That's so sweet of him."

Eli got up from the bed. "Send him in."

"Yo." Max called out to Hadrian as he opened the door wider so that Hadrian could enter the bedroom.

Eli motioned for Hadrian to take the chair that sat by the bedside.

Hadrian sat down in the offered chair. "I wanted to come by and see how you were feeling."

"I'm doing okay." She placed the empty bowl on the nightstand and folded her hands in her lap. Her hand wandered up to her hair and she made a futile attempt to make herself look presentable. "I'm grateful that you came to help."

Eli stood at the foot of the bed with his hands across his chest. "Yes, we're both really appreciative..." He was going to say more, but Max poked his head back in the room.

"Phaedra says she needs us in the library."

Eli looked torn. "I can't leave Willow alone."

Hadrian stuck his hand up. "I'm here. I can sit with her until you return." He offered. He turned to Willow. "If you're alright with that."

"I'd love that." She smiled at Hadrian before addressing Eli. "Go take care of whatever you need to do. I know it's important."

He came over and kissed her on top of the head.

"Thank you." He shook Hadrian's hand before leaving the bedroom with Max.

"Eli mentioned that Lysander was here too. Did Arsenio come as well?" She was fond of the big bear of a man and his penchant for useless historical facts.

"No, I'm afraid it was just my brother and I." Hadrian looked distracted for a minute.

The sound of the front door closing could be heard as Eli and Max left the apartment. They fell into a companionable silence. After a few minutes, Hadrian leaned forward in his chair. "I didn't want to say anything while Eli was here, because I didn't want to upset him, but I think I can help you."

She turned hopeful eyes on him. "What do you mean?"

"I have a spell that could rid you of Morgana and make everything better."

Willow felt hope grow and blossom in her chest. She wanted that more than anything. She knew that's what Phaedra, Max and Eli were going to the library for, to research spells that would get rid of Morgana for good. If Hadrian had already found a way she was up for trying anything.

"Yes. Yes. Please do it."

CHAPTER 19

Eli

PHAEDRA HAD ALREADY pulled some of the ancient spell books with Enid's help when he and Max arrived at the library. She plopped down a bunch of heavy, dusty books and some scrolls on his side of the table. Max pulled one of the scrolls so he could help.

"Who's watching Willow?" She asked the question with her head stuck in a book.

"Hadrian." Eli was already flipping through the pages of a thick tome. "He offered to sit with her. I'm sure she'll enjoy his company."

"I've been here looking for a while. Hopefully, with you guys here we can cover more ground." Phaedra jotted down some notes and then kept reading.

They'd only been at their research for about ten minutes when Lysander walked in.

"Hey."

"Hey." Phaedra and Max said in unison without bothering to look up from whatever they were reading.

Eli pulled his head out of his book. "Hi." He shook Lysander's hand.

"Could we talk for a second?" He looked over at Phaedra and Max who still hadn't glanced up from their research. "Alone?"

Even though the conversation was going to take him away from research he desperately needed to do if he was going to save Willow and his daughter, he got up from the table and followed Lysander to a back corner of the library. Lysander had never been one to make small talk or really talk to him at all, so he found himself intrigued by what he was going to say.

Once they were alone, Lysander seemed unsure about what he was going to say or how he was going to say it. "I know we haven't always seen eye to eye... and I know I'm not the best at expressing my... feelings..." He paused. "But I did want to tell you how sorry I was for everything that you and Willow are having to deal with."

Lysander surprised him. He seemed really affected by their plight. Eli found it rather touching. "I really appreciate that. I'm sure Willow will too... if that's all, I really should get back to it." He went to walk past Lysander to rejoin them at the table and continue his research.

"Yeah, sorry. I just wanted you to know I'll help in anyway I can. I know it's what Hyacinth would have wanted me to do."

Eli stopped in his tracks and turned to Lysander with a confused look on his face. How would he know what Willow's mother would have wanted? "Did Hadrian tell you that?"

Lysander looked at him strangely. "Why would my brother tell me that?"

"Don't take this the wrong way, but I just don't understand how you would know what she would have wanted. Hadrian was the one that was seeing her."

Shock was evident on Lysander's face. "What?"

Eli realized that he must have been surprised that Willow found out about Hadrian and her mother. "Oh. You didn't realize she knew about them. Willow saw the two of them together in a vision, when we were at the ruins."

"I thought she could only see the future?" He stared at Eli with puzzlement and fascination co-mingling on his face.

"She had a vision when she touched the ruin of Tholos. She said it showed her a vision of her mother with Hadrian, kissing and enjoying a day of sightseeing." Lysander's face had taken on a weird look. It almost seemed like nostalgia. "You okay?" Eli put his hand on his shoulder to pull him out of whatever thought he was having.

"That wasn't Hadrian..." Sadness filled his eyes. "I was the one who was in the relationship with Hyacinth."

Eli shook his head. What game was he playing at? "No, it was Hadrian. Willow saw him."

The short, gruff, condescending laugh that Lysander gave had Eli wanting to kick his teeth in. "Hadrian and I are identical twins. It would be easy to mistake us." He grew serious. "I assure you I was Hyacinth's lover... she was the love of my life." His tone was wistful and somber, like he was remembering their time together.

What?

Before Eli could say anything else or ask any more questions, Lysander kept talking. "We were very much in love... almost from the minute we saw each other. I never believed in love at first sight, but I have to say that's exactly what it was..." His eyes took on a faraway look. Then his eyes turned glassy, as more memories of the two of them seemed to flood his mind. He knew that look; it was the look of a man in love. It had been Lysander that was her lover. It made sense now. That day at the ruins when Willow convulsed on the ground as she had a vision, Lysander could only have recognized it for what it was if he'd seen it first hand. Hyacinth more than likely had experienced visions in front of him.

Lysander cleared his throat. "It ripped my heart out when I lost her. I was all set to join her here in the U.S.

when I got the call that she'd been killed in an accident. That's why I was so standoffish with Willow the day we met. I wasn't trying to be rude..." He swallowed. "It was just too much seeing her. She looked so much like Hyacinth. It brought up all these old emotions and feelings I hadn't felt in a very long time. There's not a day that goes by that I don't think about her."

"There's something I don't understand then..." Even as he said the words, he was still trying to make sense of it. "Why would your brother tell Willow that he was the one in the relationship with her if it was you?" Eli was starting to get a bad feeling in his gut.

Lysander scratched his head. "That doesn't make any sense. Are you sure he said that?" The confusion had him talking to himself. "Why would he say that?"

Slowly, recognition crept across his face. An ugly realization seemed to take shape, because his eyes held worry and shock. Eli wondered if the same seed that had been planted in his mind moments ago was now planted in Lysander's.

"Back when I planned to leave Greece and the coven to be with Hyacinth, my brother flew into a rage unlike anything I'd ever seen. I just assumed it was over me leaving and being so far away from him. As twins we'd always had a tight bond. I chalked it up to him not wanting to be separated by the great distance... Now when I think about it, he never really seemed to warm to her." He glanced at Eli. "Hyacinth died a few days after our fight. I was grieving so heavily that I didn't see it at the time, but he never showed any sorrow that I'd just lost her... I mean he was there for me, but..." It was evident that Lysander was trying to make sense of it all and process things he'd never taken a careful look at in the past.

"It's just, they ruled it an accident... I never thought anything of it..." Whatever part of Lysander that was trying to suppress ill thoughts about Hadrian lost the fight. "Oh no..."

Alarm bells were going off in Eli's head. His body went rigid with fear and adrenaline. The only reason that Hadrian would keep that big of a lie going is because he was hiding something. There was a time when he would have never thought anyone he cared about capable of such vile things, but if Morgana had taught him one thing, it was that anyone was capable of anything and right now Hadrian seemed to want Willow dead because she was her mother's daughter.

"I just left your psychotic brother alone with my wife. And I think we're both on the same page that he doesn't mean her any good."

CHAPTER 20

Willow

WAS IT SUPPOSED to hurt this much? "AAAHHH!" She screamed in agony. If this spell was supposed to rid her of Morgana, it felt like it was going to kill her first before that could happen. Hadrian stood on the side of the bed with his hands a few inches over her belly, chanting a spell.

She gripped the pillow and cried out again. Something didn't feel right. Sweat dripped from her brow and she clutched her stomach. The spell felt like it was going to rip her apart from the inside out. The baby was kicking against her.

"Stop!" She screamed at Hadrian. "I think..." She gritted her teeth against the pain and then said the next words through clenched teeth. "I think... the spell... is... hurting the baby." Her closed fist struck the mattress over and over as her back arched off the bed. Her head was thrown back on the pillow, her mouth was parted in a silent scream and tears leaked out of her eyes. The pain was tremendous. Had Hadrian not heard her? He wasn't stopping. She yelled once more. Her body wouldn't be able to stand much more.

Suddenly, the front door burst open and Eli and Lysander stopped short in the bedroom doorway. Both men moved slowly as they entered the room and stood on the opposite side of the bed facing Hadrian.

Eli had a thunderous look on his face and raised his hand to blast Hadrian. She wanted to call out to him, but the pain she was experiencing was too great. To him it probably looked like he was hurting her. She should have told him before she agreed. She should have involved him; he was her husband and the father. He was going to be upset with her.

Lysander placed himself between Eli and his brother. Something wasn't right.

"It's... okay." She managed to get the words out.

"Stop." Lysander had his hands raised against his brother like he was going to use his magic against him.

Hadrian continued to perform his spell, ignoring his brother's command.

"ARE YOU HURT? DID HE HURT YOU?" Eli entered her mind. By the tone in his voice she could tell he was trying hard to mask his fear.

"OF COURSE, HE DIDN'T HURT ME. HE'S TRYING TO GET RID OF MORGANA..." Even as she said the words, she wasn't sure she believed them. Hadrian hadn't stopped when she told him and Eli and Lysander were now in the room treating him like he was the enemy. "I DON'T UNDERSTAND. WHAT'S GOING ON?" She wasn't sure about anything anymore.

Before Eli could answer her, Lysander spoke to his brother again. "Why brother?" His voice was filled with anguish and she could see the tears in his eyes. *Why is he upset with Hadrian?* The pain was muddling her brain.

Hadrian did not look up when his brother spoke. It felt like he was pouring all of his energy into the spell. After a few more agonizing seconds, he stopped chanting, but his hands were still poised over her belly, the spell still working. The pain lessened some without the effect of the words, but not by much.

"You were going to choose her over me and the coven. That bitch was going to take you away from me. It wouldn't have been right. She wasn't a witch."

An evil gleam shone in Hadrian's eyes that she'd never seen before. "The thought of you cross-breeding with her and creating some kind of abomination sickened me. I had to put an end to it." He looked her straight in the eye when he said it. Her blood ran cold and for a minute her pain was forgotten as she realized that not only was Hadrian not here to help her, he was one of those supernaturals against hybrids people. She'd trusted him.

She hadn't expected to feel the sting of betrayal as acutely as she felt Morgana's, but this cut deep. He'd loved her mother... hadn't he?

"I won't let you kill her too." Lysander vowed. His hands were still raised against his brother.

"End him or I will." Eli's voice was deadly as he raised his hands and stepped around Lysander. "If something happens to her or my kid, so help me..." The threat of retribution hung in the air.

"See. They're trying to come between us again. First, it was her mother and now it's her. She's even worse than her mother: Oracle and part fae." He spit the words out like she had some sort of disease or infection that was catching. "Why couldn't she just die the first time I tried to kill her?" He never let up with the spell.

The room went quiet at his admission.

"The first time?" Lysander sputtered out.

"I came here the day before her wedding and tried to kill the baby then, then again when I danced with her, and nothing, but now I know why... Morgana."

Her head was swimming. She felt like such a fool. This whole time she'd been treating him like some sort of father figure, because she believed he loved her mother and twice he'd attempted to destroy her child, because of some sick, twisted, ignorant bigoted belief he held. No. She was pissed. This bastard would not kill her baby or her.

A roar tore from her throat and she mustered what strength she could, the kind of strength that sits in reserves for just this sort of thing: kicking ass when you have nothing left, but you're mad as hell. Hadrian was launched off his feet and thrown into the dresser by her faery blast. She sat up as she kept blasting him, longer than she needed to. When she stopped, she glared at him, wishing her eyes could spit fireballs at him. "How's that for part fae, you fucker." The adrenaline coursed through her veins for a few more seconds as she watched Hadrian's unconscious body slump to the ground. Her faery blast sputtered out and she fell back onto the bed.

Eli was beside her in an instant. "Willow."

Sheer exhaustion weighed on every limb, every part of her being. "I'm okay." She felt around her belly, needing to feel the baby kick. Panic started to choke her as her hands frantically moved around on her belly waiting for a movement, a kick, anything that would indicate she was still alive. *Please!*

"What's wrong? Are you hurt?" His eyes searched her over, looking for an injury or wound. Lysander had come to stand near his brother's comatose body. He hung back.

"I can't feel the baby." She stood right at the borderline of hysterics. *Please!* Her fingers probed and jabbed at her stomach, praying for the baby to give her some sort of indication that she was still alive.

Out of the corner of her eye, she could see Eli wringing his hands. The helplessness she glimpsed for a brief moment had her averting her gaze. No. Not right now. *Keep your shit together.*

She held her breath and her fingers continued to dance across her belly. "C'mon Lily." She hadn't yet discussed the name with Eli, but that's what she'd been calling her the last few days when she whispered to her while she was confined to the bed. The tears burned to get out. Despair was sitting on her shoulder, waiting to cover her like a blanket. She was ready to let the grief wash over her and carry her away. She was ready to concede... until she felt a tiny motion.

Her mouth dropped open and she pushed her hand on the area she believed the motion had come from and in response Lily kicked against it. Shocked relief washed over her and opened the floodgates. "She's alive." She grabbed Eli's hand, as happy tears flowed down her cheeks, and pressed it to her belly. Lily kicked again. Eli gasped when he felt his daughter and grinned broadly at Willow. "She's alive." He repeated. Neither of them could stop grinning at the other like a fool. Without another word, Eli buried his face in her neck and held her. She clung to him. They were all still alive.

CHAPTER 21

Eli

THE VERY NEXT day, after he was sure that Willow and the baby would be okay while he was away, they transported Hadrian to Las Vegas, where the Congress of Supernatural Beings convened. His father and Lysander were also with him. The Protectors had stayed behind to do their part in figuring out how to save Lily. While Phaedra, Zoriana and Max scoured the library for a spell that would rid them of Morgana once and for all, he'd left Evie and Delaney at the apartment to watch out for his family.

Last night, during Hadrian's stay in the Walker house dungeon, he, Phaedra and Lysander had woken him up and administered a truth spell to make him talk. They knew he wasn't in it alone and wanted answers about who else was part of the Supernaturals Against Hybrids group.

Hadrian did his best to resist the effects of the spell, but ended up giving up Damaris, one of the maenads. He remembered when Willow thought they were sleeping together. Appearances could be deceiving. They were just together all the time, because they were in cahoots. The other witches and supernaturals he'd mentioned thankfully hadn't been anyone else he knew, but it was bad enough that any of them thought like that.

Lysander hadn't said much between last night and this morning when they teleported to Vegas. He was sure it couldn't have been easy to learn that your brother was the one responsible for killing the love of your life. There were times he thought about asking if the man wanted to talk about it, but they were not close and part of him doubted there would ever be more than just a cordial respect, no matter what he'd been to Willow's mother.

Eli turned his mind back to the matter at hand. It was a good thing Congress was in session. If not, they would have had to hold Hadrian for another month before they could ask for an audience. He was anxious to get this over with and get back. Being away from Willow and Lily made him antsy, given everything that was going on, but he needed to speak to Congress and make them understand they needed to treat the people that thought this way like terrorists.

He'd always had an issue with the Congress. Yes, it was great to have a governing body that allowed for all supernaturals to come together and have themselves heard, but it was often problematic. There was no term of office. You could occupy a seat on Congress for as long as you lived, unopposed.

The building that held the Congress of Supernatural Beings looked like any other random utility company to most. Inside there was an area to "pay your bill". The counter was usually where a supernatural filed a grievance, complaint or concern. Occasionally, they got a lost human stray and they just redirected them to another building. If Congress was in session, there was another entrance you were escorted to if you had business. Today, that's the entrance they were using.

Eli shoved Hadrian past the entrance. He sported anti-magic cuffs to keep him from being able to escape. Arsenio had rounded up the other members of Hadrian's hate group, along with Damaris and would be meeting them here shortly.

Once inside, after walking down a long hallway, you entered a room that resembled the United Nations. Around the room, rows and rows of chairs sat behind desks that held name placards and microphones. People were milling about or in conversation. Others sat at their seats writing or on their phones.

They followed his father to a section of the room that was marked for the witch delegation. After he sat the prisoner down, he dropped into a seat next to him and Lysander took the seat on the other side. His father wondered off to be the born politician that he was.

Eli glanced around to see who had shown up. He'd only attended Congress a handful of times. This was the first time he'd come with an issue. He got the sense that he was being watched. The hairs on the back of his neck stood on end. He became more alert as he looked around... then their eyes met. Aine Sparklefrost, queen of the faeries. She'd been a leader in the Congress well before he was born. No one was certain of her age, which was normally the case with faeries. Her eyes were locked on his. The expression on her face was unreadable.

Aine was an attractive woman, if you went for that lethal, femme fatale vibe. She had long, lavender hair, lavender eyes and dressed between a mixture of glam and biker chic. The otherworldly presence and Irish lilt were very soothing, but he knew faeries could be anything but. None of her trickery worked on him. He knew everything about her was meant to lull you into a false sense of security: the voice, the eyes, her appearance.

Although he'd come to trust Cosmo, as much as one could trust a faery, there was something that put him on edge with Aine. He knew that faeries had the ability to change their appearance in an instant, especially to make themselves look human, but amongst other supernaturals they usually preferred to look like themselves.

There were so many species of faeries that they hadn't even all been accounted for yet. Not all of them were cute sprites and pixies or sexy nymphs; some species were hideous hobgoblins or gremlins. For all he knew, the appearance the faery queen sported right now was a lie, just one of her many disguises. She was smart enough to know that this appearance was far more attractive and acceptable. No one knew what classification of faery she actually belonged too.

Thanks to her, the faeries had done a good job with making sure the Congress hadn't passed a law to force them to classify themselves. Just one of many issues he took with Congress.

He broke eye contact first and leaned back in his seat. When was this thing going to get started so he could get the hell out of here?

Once the session got underway it was a bit of a snooze fest. Eventually, the witch who headed up their delegation, a woman from a coven in Japan he wasn't acquainted with, introduced him and Lysander by yielding the floor to them.

It was clear that Lysander had done this before as he maneuvered the microphone so it sat in front of him. Eli was too glad to sit back and let him do the bulk of the talking. Halfway through Lysander's talk about more enforcement against hate groups like Supernaturals Against Hybrids, Aine interrupted him.

"I would love to hear from Mr. Walker about this, since it was his wife that was the target of this group."

Lysander moved the microphone in front of him and motioned for him to sit up straighter and address the audience.

He leaned forward. "What do you want to know? Lysander's pretty much covered it." He was too tired and angry to be here, dealing with this right now.

She cocked her head and looked at him like he was a smudge on her Prada boot she needed to wipe off. "Many of us haven't been faced with these...problems. Why should we, as a whole, make this our fight?"

Was he hearing her correctly? Now he was amped up and angrier than he'd been before. "So, what you're saying is unless it's happening to you, you don't see the need for stricter punishments for these types of crimes? Listen, this is everyone's problem, just because it isn't knocking on your door today, doesn't mean you won't be affected by it at some point." He knew he shouldn't be getting worked up, but he was so agitated by her callousness.

Underneath the table he balled his fist up in anger. "I thought the whole supernatural Congress was about uniting together as one against a common enemy. Or is that only what you do when it serves you?" He looked directly at her. "When it's your family fighting for their life, you let me know what you would and wouldn't do, which fights you'd pick and choose to involve yourself in..."

"Let's go take a walk son..." His father kept trying to pull him up from the chair and away from the microphone.

Before his father could force him to leave, he got in one more potshot. "Oh, and in case someone here hadn't passed on the memo to you. My wife is part fae, so yeah, I guess that would concern you a little bit, make it your fight too, since she is one of you." He looked at her pointedly. His angry gaze burning into her.

"Ok, let's get some air." His father said more firmly as he pulled him down the aisle, not giving him the opportunity to pause.

When they finally got outside, he ripped his arm away from his father and paced the sidewalk. "Did she really just ask why it was everyone's problem?" He wasn't expecting an answer. The need to blow off steam, punch something, anything, was so strong he wanted to scream.

"I know how angry... how powerless..."

Eli exploded and jabbed his finger in his father's face. "Don't talk to me about feeling powerless..." He got in his dad's face. It wasn't him he was angry with, but he was the one that was there so he got to be the punching bag. "I need a good whipping boy so you'll have to do. Why did you pull me out of there? Did you hear the crap that was coming out of her mouth?"

His father didn't seem fazed one bit by his tantrum. "This is politics. You don't win people over by emotion..."

"You mean you don't win those people…" he roughly stabbed his finger in the direction of the building that housed Congress. "You don't win those people over by emotion. I'm flesh and blood." He beat his fists against his chest to make his point. "I have emotions. One of which is anger. I don't know anyone that wouldn't be feeling the way I am if their family was in danger and some jackass asked why they should be concerned."

His father was trying his best to de-escalate the situation, but it wasn't working. "I'm not saying you're wrong. You just have to deal with them a certain way to get things done… She was out of line."

"Why weren't you saying that in there? Instead of pulling me out like I'd done something wrong? Fuck them." He put his hands on top of his head and huffed as he resumed his pacing.

The remainder of the session, he waited outside. He sat with his back against the wall of the building with his arms resting on his elbows.

"You okay?"

He looked up to find Lysander standing over him. "How'd it go in there?"

Lysander looked away. "Hadrian's going to be executed for his crimes in a few days… I'll come back and be a witness."

It was clear there were many emotions and feelings the man was trying to hold back for his sake, but he couldn't be upset with Lysander for wanting and needing to mourn his brother, no matter how atrocious his crimes were. It was his brother, his twin brother. There were conflicting emotions there, given Hadrian was responsible for killing the love of his life and totally changing the path he'd seen for himself. Lysander collected himself and turned back to Eli. He reached out his hand to help Eli up to his feet.

Eli said the only thing he could think to say. "I need to get home to my girls."

"Let's go."

CHAPTER 22

Willow

WILLOW'S PALMS WERE splayed flat across her belly as she crooned the old jazz standard, "Come Rain Or Come Shine," to Lily. The bath seemed to relax them both. Morgana seemed to be giving her a bit of a reprieve. She hadn't had any excruciating pains since early yesterday, before all the craziness with Hadrian.

Just as she was finishing the song, Eli stepped in the doorway, applauding her performance. She smiled up at him. "Looks like daddy liked the song too." She whispered loudly to Lily.

For a moment, it felt normal. She forgot about the warlock's spirit trying to take her daughter, she forgot about how just last night she had to defend against a hateful witch because her and her baby were hybrids. Right now, he was just her husband, coming home to her, after a long day to find her taking a bath.

"Hey." Eli wore a tired smile as he leaned against the doorframe taking her in.

Her breasts and belly bobbed on top of the water in invitation. Like a moth being drawn to a flame, he moved towards the tub and sunk to his knees. He planted his hands on the edge and leaned in and kissed her. It felt like a lifetime ago that they'd been able to just act like horny newlyweds.

She cupped his face in her hands and kissed him back. Water sloshed over the side of the tub as she tugged him by his shirt and pulled him closer. When his hand dipped beneath the water she spread her legs as wide as she could against the tub, trying to give him better access. As his fingers teased and stroked her lips, she groaned into his mouth.

After another minute or so, he pulled away first. Dazedly, he licked his lips and peered at her. The front of his shirt was soaked. He hadn't removed his hand from between her legs. Their eyes stayed locked on each other as two of his fingers slid in and out of her pussy. Willow gyrated her hips, wanting to be filled even more. Her mouth hung open in ecstasy. It wasn't long and she was coming, moaning out her pleasure. While her body shook from the orgasm he'd wrung from it, he leaned over and kissed her mouth once more.

"We could run another bath... and you could join me this time?" She ran her fingers up and down his arm.

His desire for her had made her feel beautiful and wanted, something she hadn't felt since all this began. It warmed her insides to know that he still wanted her and now that she'd had a taste of it, she wanted to keep enjoying it all night long and not be consumed with thoughts of what tomorrow would bring.

The lust cleared from his eyes. "Oh baby..." He sighed. "When I came in here and saw you like that I got sidetracked. Lysander's waiting to see you." He leaned in and pressed his forehead against hers. "I promise once he leaves... I'm all yours."

He kissed her nose and reached for a towel. "Let me help you." As he dried her off, she felt slight disappointment that they wouldn't be going straight to the bedroom. The only thing that kept it from being full-blown disappointment was that she was curious about what Lysander had to say.

After she dressed, she went into the living room where Lysander was waiting. The minute she entered he stood. The gesture was very old-fashioned. When she sat, he also sat back down. His demeanor was different than the way he usually treated her, which bordered on cold.

Eli moved into the kitchen so they could be alone.

"First, I wanted to apologize again for my brother. I'm very sorry about what happened."

She wasn't sure what to say to that so she said nothing.

"I wanted to come here, because I felt that I owed you an explanation for my behavior..." He swallowed. "Yesterday, Eli told me that you believed Hadrian was the one your mother had been with and when you confronted Hadrian about that he didn't clear up the error... I was your mother's lover... She was the love of my life."

For the first time, since she'd met him, she saw a glimpse of his emotions that he kept hidden behind the stoic mask. She was reminded of the way he looked in the vision: young, carefree... happy. Hadrian had robbed them both of her mother's love. She reached over and placed her hand on his. He looked at her and smiled.

"When I saw you for the first time in Greece, coming up the walkway towards me, I thought I was seeing a ghost. I was shocked by how much you looked like her. You were a living, breathing reminder of what I'd lost. I did not mean to be rude to you. It was just painful, because all of the memories I buried away resurfaced." Lysander placed his other hand over top of hers.

"Will you tell me how you fell in love?" She realized what she was asking. "If it's too painful to talk about. I understand."

"No. It's the least I can do. It would give me great pleasure to talk about your mother." He scooted closer to her. "I never believed in love at first sight and then I met your mother. She walked into the coven with some of her Protectors, and our eyes met across the room and it was instant." His eyes took on a wistful, faraway look. "It was like her soul reached out across the divide to mine and I just knew I wanted to spend the rest of my life with her. We spent two glorious weeks together. I showed her around Delphi."

He chuckled at some forgotten memory. "We did all the romantic, touristy things together." It was nice to see the smile on his face. Smiling made him look ten years younger. She could see why her mother had fallen for him.

"In one of the letters my mother wrote to me, she mentioned that you were going to come back with her."

"I was supposed to come back with her and then your mother asked me to give her a couple days, before I followed. It was the one and only argument we had, because I wanted to get on the plane with her. After knowing what I know now...I'm wondering if I'd gotten on that plane with her, and gone to the U.S. right away as planned, if I'd been able to save her?" Sorrow welled up in his eyes and the look he gave her made her heartache. It almost seemed like he was asking her for forgiveness.

A realization struck Willow. She remembered her mother on the videotape and how she spoke of her own death. Then she remembered the line from the letter: *There's someone I want you to meet. I'm not certain you'll get the opportunity and that makes me sad, because I think you'd like him if you did.* "Actually, I forgot something she mentioned in the letter... My mother was sad. She wanted me to meet you, but she didn't think I would..." She took both of Lysander's hands in hers.

"Lysander, I think my mother knew she was going to die. She may have even known when and how. It's a possibility if you'd come home with her, maybe you would have died too and she was trying to save you..."

Now she realized, all the brooding, anger and silence was part grief, part guilt. "I think you've blamed yourself for a long time for my mother's death and you shouldn't." She squeezed his hands. "She loved you and I know she would have wanted you to have a full, happy life... even if that did not include her."

"Eíste i kóri tis mitéras sas." The smile he bestowed on her lit up his whole face. When he spoke in his mother tongue, Greek, she was fascinated and curious by what he'd said. Before she could open her mouth to ask the question, a pain unlike any other ripped through her abdomen. The pain was horrendous. Breath would not escape her. She couldn't scream. She pitched forward and almost fell to the ground, but Lysander caught her.

"Eli!" Lysander yelled.

He rushed into the room and both men knelt beside her. Through the pain, she looked up at Eli. He gripped her hand between both of his strong, powerful hands. She was terrified, would this be the time the pain killed her? What about Lily? More stabbing pains pierced her abdomen and finally she threw her head back and cried out.

CHAPTER 23

Eli

THE BOOK WENT sailing across the room, to join the others that were in a pile in the corner of the library. He was sure that Enid would not appreciate the way he was handling the spell books, some of which were ancient, but he didn't care.

Eventually, Zoriana put Willow to sleep, when the pain wouldn't stop. The sleep-inducing spell had knocked her out. He was so grateful she wasn't in pain anymore, but the echoes of her torment still raged in his head.

He opened up another book and did his best to expel the haunting sound.

"Anything?" Max asked Phaedra after shutting his latest book. The two of them had practically lived in the library since finding out what they faced.

She didn't respond, which caused both of them to look over at her.

"Phaedra?" Eli was concerned. Had Phaedra finally snapped? He knew she was running on very little sleep after being the one spearheading the search. He'd been in and out dealing with the hate group situation and then doing his best to take care of Willow. He knew she'd shouldered a lot of the responsibility and for that he was grateful.

He waved his hand in between her and the book. "Phaedra?"

She looked up from the book. "I think I've found the solution."

His face lit up. "Seriously?" He was a millisecond away from picking her up from the chair and hugging her.

It didn't sit well that Phaedra's face wasn't lit up in a grin. "I don't think you're going to like it."

He came back down off of his high. *Why does there always have to be a catch?*

"What am I not going to like?" He sat back in his chair and crossed his arms over his chest, waiting for her to deliver the bad news. He knew he could count on her not to sugar coat anything.

Phaedra rested the book on the table. "We have two options. One is better than the other, but is very risky. Do you want the good news or bad news first?"

She sounded like she was already trying to talk him out of it. Phaedra had never been one to skirt around an issue. Why was she doing it now? "Just tell me."

She looked at him pointedly. "Good news or bad news, Elias?"

He huffed. "Good news."

Her gaze shifted to Max before she turned back to Eli and took a deep breath. She clasped her hands together on the table in front of her. " I... we..." She amended her words. "We've scoured pretty much every book over the last few days and there isn't a spell that I think is strong enough on its own to get rid of Morgana..."

"That's supposed to be your good news?" Eli stood up so quickly from the chair, it clattered to the ground."

"Stop yelling. I haven't gotten to any news yet. Let me finish." She rolled her eyes as he picked up the chair and sat back down.

"Because there isn't a spell. The first option would involve as many of the witches in the coven as we could get, trying to perform an exorcism. We would probably need to reach out to some in other covens to volunteer..." She paused.

"I hear a but coming, so what is it?" Eli placed his elbows on the table and waited.

"Even with all of that, there is no guarantee that it will work, because as Morgana stated, she has a lot of power behind her."

He let out of breath. "What's the bad news?" Exasperation was all he could feel, even before Phaedra opened her mouth to tell him the so-called bad news. It was sounding pretty bleak and hopeless. He rested his head in his hands.

"So... you mentioned that your father said Morgana was using siphoner magic. What if we took it away?"

"How would we do that?" His head was still buried in his hands as he asked the question.

"We cut off her ancestral magic. We cut her ties to the ancestors. Because she's in spirit form, it wouldn't be the same as stripping. We would talk directly to the ancestors to ask them to revoke her access. They in turn could help block her access even to the black magic she has access to..."

The smile was plastered to his face before he'd fully lifted his head all the way. "That's genius."

"Don't... there's more and you're not going to like it." Phaedra was very serious.

A sick feeling sat in his gut. *Why couldn't it ever just be easy?* "Rip off the band-aid."

Pity clouded Phaedra's eyes. The impact of it almost made him look away, but he didn't.

"In order for this to work we would need to strip Lily of her ancestral magic, because even if we cut off Morgana's direct access, she could still siphon magic through Lily, still giving her access to the ancestors."

It felt like he'd been gut punched and had the breath knocked from his lungs once Phaedra mentioned that part of the plan. She must have seen the shock register on his face, because she rushed on to conclude what the plan would entail.

"Once neither of them had anymore ties to the ancestors it should be no problem to exorcise her..." She watched his face very carefully when she said the next part. "What you must know by now is that there would be no guarantee that one or both would survive."

For a minute, he just sat there. Her words were replaying themselves in his head: *What you must know by now is that there would be no guarantee that one or both would survive.*

The only thing his mind could think of in that moment was the tiny body of his daughter writhing in agony as her soul was pulled apart during the stripping and what in turn that would do to Willow since she still carried her. The recollection of how his psyche had felt torn and shredded during the process still woke him on some nights, even though he'd never told anyone that. It was something that you never forgot.

When he finally found his voice it was eerily calm at first. "You want me to put my little baby girl, my unborn daughter through the stripping process? Are you fucking serious?" The last words came out through clenched teeth.

"That alone could kill her. I'm a grown man, do you know what that almost did to me?" His hands kept opening and closing into fists as he tried to gain control of his anger. He knew that Phaedra was just the messenger, but his blood boiled at the prospect of subjecting his baby to that horror.

"You want to traumatize her before she even comes out of the womb?" He wiped his hand over his face. "Then you sit here and tell me that there's no guarantee that either of them might live and I'm supposed to go along with this?" All the anger and rage he was feeling about the situation had to come out in some sort of way. His fists came down on the table with a loud bang, rattling the books and cups that sat on top of it. Needing to release even more of the fury that he felt, he stood and booted his chair across the room.

After destroying a few more pieces of furniture, he came back to the table where Phaedra and Max sat in silence.

"No." His eyes didn't meet either one of theirs. "We'll have to make it work with option number one." Without getting a response, he turned and left the room.

When he returned to his apartment, Zoriana must have realized he wasn't in the mood for small talk or answering any questions. Once she left, he stripped off his clothes and crawled into bed with Willow. She was still under the sleep-inducing spell. Carefully, he undressed her and then positioned her on her side so she was facing him. Eli looked down at her sleeping face and stroked her cheek. He leaned in and kissed her forehead and then placed a lingering kiss on her lips. His hands went to her belly. "I love you both so much." The murmured words were whispered into the dark, before he curled his body around hers, keeping Lily between them.

If it was going to be his last night with his family, he wanted to feel both their heartbeats against his. As he held the two women he loved against his heart, he sang The Cure's "Lovesong".

***

The next morning everyone was waiting on them. He had taken his time when he woke up. Wanting to be with her and Lily as much as possible before the exorcism... just in case.

It had been agreed upon that Willow wouldn't be woken up until she was within the circle of the pentacle, that way her body wouldn't have to endure any unnecessary stress until she absolutely had to. He wished she could sleep through it all, but that just wasn't an option.

All eyes were on them, once he stepped into the room carrying her in his arms. He didn't turn to look at or acknowledge anyone. He kept his gaze focused on the pentacle with the crystals surrounding it. Anyone in his way quickly stepped out of it. Gently, he lay Willow in the center of the pentacle. Before he stepped away from her unconscious body he kissed her forehead.

The minute he stepped outside the circle, some of the other witches began to walk in circles around the pentacle and chant protection spells.

CHAPTER 24

Willow

THE AGONY BEGAN before she could open her eyes. "Make it stop!" She wailed. Her eyes flew open as she heard the chanting. *How did I get here?* Frantically, she searched the room, twisting this way and that looking for Eli. She couldn't find him. All the witches were wearing their robes with the symbols on them. Everyone looked alike in her blurry, unfocused vision. Tears swam in her eyes.

A fresh wave of pain hit her again and she shut her eyes to it. Why was he letting her go through this alone? Where was he?

She knew her thinking was irrational, but she was in so much pain that only seemed to lessen for seconds, before new pains gripped her again.

"Eli." She mumbled too low to be heard over the chanting.

The chanting changed and the lit candles flickered during the incantation. She wasn't sure what was being said, but whatever they were doing was pissing Morgana off. The evil witch was flaying every nerve ending she could with an immense amount of pain. Willow howled while her body contorted and thrashed against the ground. Even Killian's torture had never felt like this. In the midst of all of it, all she could think about as her brain turned in on itself and tried to block the pain was how much she wanted her mother, even though her mother was dead and hadn't been able to hold her in a very long time.

She clutched her stomach hoping that Lily wasn't feeling and experiencing all of this too. For a brief moment the pain let up and she turned onto her side gasping for breath, but just as quickly it resumed. It felt like Morgana had turned up the pain factor. The witches chanting got louder. Her body felt like it was burning up from the inside out. The throbbing and stabbing pain in her head felt like it would cleave her skull in two at any moment. She was seeing stars and her eyes weren't even closed.

She wanted to yell at them to stop, because every time they chanted the pain intensified. The strangled sob that was being wrenched from her body was going to choke her. She was choking on her own fear. Her body convulsed and her eyes rolled back into her head.

Willow couldn't take anymore. Her spirit willingly left her body.

Was she dead? She looked down and realized she was looking down at her body... her spirit was floating over her body. *What have I done?*

Eli rushed towards the circle. A few of the witches, including Phaedra, tried to pull him back. They kept him from entering, but he shook them off and got down on his hands and knees, laying flat on his stomach, on the opposite side of the pentacle from where her limp body lay. "I know you can hear me baby, so I need you to listen to me... You are the strongest, bravest woman I know. I've seen you face rejection, fall down and get back up so many times, suffer mental and physical torture. I've seen you take a spear through the side and survive, a knife to the gut; you've been dead and come back to life... so I need you to fight. Fight for yourself. Fight for me... Fight for Lily. Fight for us... Baby, I need you to come back to me. Please." Tears gathered in the corners of his eyes.

For a while he just lay there. The room was silent. There were a few sniffles and some people were softly crying.

"Damn it Willow!" He pounded his hand on the floor. "Fight! You're a fighter! You fight! You here me."

His pleas made her cry. She didn't want to leave him or Lily, but she was so tired.

"You're not dead. You just needed a break." The voice came out of nowhere. She turned around and around trying to find the source. Why did the voice sound so familiar? Where had the voice come from?

"Who are you? Where are you?" She kept whipping her head, this way and that, wondering if she'd imagined it.

"I'm here."

She looked up above her and fresh tears formed in her eyes. "Mom?"

Her mother's spirit was suspended in place watching her. She looked exactly like she did the last time Willow saw her. Her hair was a mess of wild curls and she was wearing the black leather jacket that Willow now owned.

Willow drew closer, forgetting for a moment about what was unfolding below her.

"You just needed a rest, baby, that's all." Her mother's smile was so bright. It beckoned her.

"Mom?" The tears fell. "Is it really you?"

Her mother nodded. "I'm here.

"How? How are you here?" She still couldn't shake the disbelief she felt.

"Mathilda." Her mother beamed at her. "She was worried about you. Said you needed me."

Willow looked down at her still unconscious body and saw Eli still begging her to wake up.

Looking back up at her mother, she begged. "I want to stay here with you."

Empathy warmed her mother's eyes and she sighed. "No, you don't, baby. That's just the pain talking." She reached out and rubbed Willow's cheek. "I raised you to be a fighter."

Her mother looked down at the scene below them. "You don't want to leave them. That little girl needs you and Eli needs you too."

"How do I fight when I'm so tired?" Even though she wasn't in her physical body, she could feel the burden and weight of everything that had led up to this moment.

"There's something I never told anyone, not even Cora. I didn't want to put it into one of the letters I left you because I was afraid of who might get a hold of them... Plus, I held out hope that maybe I'd be wrong... or maybe you'd turn it around."

"What are you talking about?" It was hard to keep the frustrated confusion from her voice. This wasn't exactly the time for riddles.

"I saw and heard this moment Willow? In color and loud and clear in stereo?"

"You could hear your visions?"

"Focus..." Briefly, her mother gave her a stern look. "I watched this moment play out so many times and the outcome was never clear to me, because you've always had a choice. Even now you have a choice. So I'm going to tell you what's about to happen and you'll have to choose how to respond."

Willow turned back around to look at the scene below. Her mother came up and stood at her back. "In a second, Morgana's spirit will realize yours has left your body and she will possess it. Which will give you a window of opportunity." Just like her mother said it would, she watched her body move and talk without her in it, as Morgana possessed her and began taunting Eli.

"I don't know whether you'll have certain victory, but you have a choice to make. You can choose to stay here, free of all the pain... or you can go back and fight, knowing that the outcome is unclear." Her mother touched her shoulder. "It's your choice."

CHAPTER 25

Eli

"PLEASE COME BACK." He muttered to her unconscious body, as he lay there on his stomach looking at her. She was so still. He couldn't tell if she was breathing or not. Had Morgana finally killed her?

The chanting had stopped and the silence in the room was deafening. Willow's arm twitched and then her eyes popped open.

"Willow?" He lifted his head up and gazed at her with a hopeful expression.

"Not today." A sinister smile that he'd never seen on Willow's face let him know that it wasn't Willow in her body, but Morgana.

He got to his feet.

"So much for your little exorcism. I guess the pain got to be too much for sweet little wifey." She mocked him while walking around the circle getting a feel for her new body.

There was no way he was going to let this bitch wear Willow's skin like she was trying on some new clothes.

"What have you done with my daughter? If you've hurt her..."

"What? What are you going to do?" They glared at each other.

Then Morgana's sinister grin was back on Willow's face. "So sweet, such a good dad. Aww... are you worried about poor little Lily?" She mocked him again by wearing a frownie face and rubbing her fists in her eyes as she pretended to cry. Just as abruptly as she made the gesture, she stopped. "Don't worry. I'm keeping her safe. Remember, I need her if I'm going to live. I can't have her traumatized before I'm able to fully take over." She sneered at him and he wanted to kill her.

He raised his hands, ready to cast his own spell on her. He'd had enough of this evil bitch.

"Uh, uh, uh." She wagged her head from side to side at him.

"You know, since I'm in Willow's body now and it appears she's not coming back. She ran like the coward that she is... I don't really need Lily anymore. I can just reside in this body." She wrapped Willow's arms around her body. "Maybe I'll just snap my fingers and get rid of the little brat."

Eli's hands dropped to his sides in defeat and he stared at her. He'd never felt such hate and disgust for someone as he did right now. "Don't." He ground out the word, hating to beg her for anything.

Morgana just continued to smile, celebrating her victory.

A thought occurred to him. Morgana had just told him that she had Lily protected. They still had one shot to take Morgana down. He turned to Phaedra. "Remember option 2?"

Surprise colored her face. "Are you sure?"

"No." He shook his head. "But, I'm all out of choices."

Phaedra raced over to some of the other witches to give the order to start talking to the ancestors to shut off Morgana's ancestral magic.

Morgana looked at him suspiciously. "What are you up to?" She walked around the circle she was trapped in. "What are they doing?"

Eli stared at her without responding. He couldn't contain the smug look that crossed his face.

Just as she was about to sneer at him again and no doubt say something to try and piss him off, she hit the ground hard, like something had fallen on her.

Willow's body rolled around on the ground and appeared to be fighting itself. Her hand went up to her throat and choked her out and the next she was punching herself in the eye. The expression she wore kept snarling and changing, smiling one minute and looking pissed off the next.

"Willow?" He didn't even try to keep the hope out of his voice.

"Yes." Willow confirmed. Only to be followed by Morgana telling him the opposite. "No."

Willow had landed back in her body and was fighting to kick Morgana out.

Adrenaline seemed to be flowing through Phaedra, just like it was flowing through him as they watched. "If Willow manages to push her out, without a host body she's vulnerable. By that time, she won't have the connection of the ancestors or black magic and we should be able to destroy her spirit once and for all. Willow just has to get out of the circle quickly once she pushes her out."

Eli turned to watch her rolling around on the floor, fighting an internal struggle for her body. "WILLOW." He pushed into her mind.

"I'M A LITTLE BUSY."

"ONCE YOU MANAGE TO PUSH HER OUT, GET OUT OF THE CIRCLE AS FAST AS YOU CAN AND WE'LL TAKE CARE OF THE REST."

For a minute there was no response, as the body continued to battle itself.

"K." She finally responded.

Several seconds later, a loud roar was heard coming out of Willow's mouth. Eli peered at Phaedra.

"Someone just lost their lifeline to the ancestors."

Now if Willow could just push her out before the Elders would have to try and strip Lily's ancestral magic.

"What about…"

He already knew what Phaedra was going to ask him. "Just hold off for a minute. Let's give Willow a chance. She may be able to push her out without us needing to resort to that."

Phaedra didn't look that certain. "We have a tiny window before Morgana realizes she still has that in reserves. I can maybe give you five minutes tops."

Eli turned away from Phaedra. He couldn't lose Lily. Willow was unaware of any of this plan. He had to tell her what they were up against. "I DON'T WANT TO INTERRUPT YOU, BUT THERE'S SOMETHING YOU NEED TO KNOW." He paused and cleared his throat. His eyes were on Willow's body, watching it wiggle and thrash around as the two souls within fought for dominance. "PART OF THE PLAN WE'RE WORKING ON TO DESTROY MORGANA, MEANS THEY WOULD NEED TO STRIP LILY OF HER ANCESTRAL MAGIC SO THAT MORGANA CAN'T SIPHON IT FROM HER AND USE IT…"

He looked back at Phaedra and then back at Willow. "I NEVER TOLD YOU WHAT STRIPPING FELT LIKE... BUT I'LL TELL YOU THAT LILY COULDN'T SURVIVE IT... IF YOU CAN'T GET MORGANA OUT OF YOUR BODY IN THE NEXT FOUR MINUTES, THEY'LL STRIP LILY'S MAGIC TO KEEP MORGANA FROM USING IT... AND IT'S A GOOD POSSIBILITY WE'LL LOSE HER."

He knew Willow had heard him, but she'd said nothing. His nerves were frayed as he continued to watch and wait. He bit his thumbnail in agitation as he tried to settle his nerves. Fear kept him from looking back at Phaedra for a time check. Nervously, he tapped his foot. "Come on baby." The words were spoken low so only he heard them.

A loud yell ripped through the air and a spirit came flying out of Willow's body. Within seconds she rolled out of the circle of the pentacle. The spirit tried to dive after her and missed her.

The only reason the spirit was even visible to the naked eye was because it was trapped in the circle of the pentacle and the crystals and unable to go anywhere.

The spirit screeched and banged against the invisible prison it found itself in. They couldn't hear it.

Eli and Phaedra ran to Willow's body, anxious to know which one was trapped. When they rolled her over, she was unconscious. He bent down to shake her awake and Phaedra had her hands poised and at the ready to defend if necessary.

"Willow?" He shook her shoulder, hoping against hope that it was Willow and that she was still alive. "Willow?" Her eyes started to flutter open. She blinked a few more times and looked up at him. "Eli." She moaned in discomfort, while clutching her belly.

"How do we know for sure it's her?" Phaedra still had her hands ready to cast a spell if there was any clue that Morgana had made it out and not Willow.

His eyes searched hers. He thought back to something from far back that only Willow would know. "That night you first learned who you were, after everyone had left, you asked me a question. Do you remember what it was?"

She managed a weak smile. "I asked you why you didn't speak to me that day in the break room at work?"

Relief flooded him as he grinned down at her. Then he glanced up at the spirit still banging on the invisible wall of the circle wanting to get out, before he turned his gaze to Phaedra. "Kill that bitch."

Phaedra gave the signal and the chanting from the witches reached a crescendo as they all chanted to destroy Morgana. Her spirit couldn't withstand the combined power of all the witches because she no longer had ancestral magic or the tie to her black magic and her spirit crumpled to the ground, before being turned to dust and disintegrated.

Eli pulled Willow onto his lap and held her. They'd survived. Both of them had survived. Soon they were surrounded by all of the Walker witches.

Willow pulled back to look at him. She was weak, tired and injured, but the radiant, triumphant smile she gave him, made his heart swell.

"I love you."

"I love you too." Eli leaned in and kissed her.

CHAPTER 26

Willow

EPILOGUE

1 YEAR LATER

"JUST PUT THE last box over there." She instructed the movers while she glanced around the living room of the new house, her, Eli and Lily had just moved into.

Eli walked through the open front door carrying a gurgling nine month old Lily in his arms. Phaedra, Max and Zoriana had either boxes or other items from the moving truck in their arms.

Willow giggled. "How did Eli end up being the one not doing anything?" She took Lily out of his arms. The little girl clapped her hands together before grabbing Willow's face. She held her daughter up above her head and cooed at her, making her giggle some more.

Her eyes lit up and sparkled with joy at hearing the tinkle of her daughter's laughter.

"Let's see if she'll come to Uncle Max." Max came up beside her and took her daughter.

"You already knew that she would because she adores you." She shook her head and went to sit on Eli's lap.

"That's everything Mr. and Mrs. Walker. We'll be going now." Some of the movers had already walked out and the last guy tipped his hat to them and went out the front door.

Max took a seat and bounced Lily on his knees.

"So… Nashville huh?" Phaedra asked while looking between the two of them.

Eli patted Willow's leg. "Yep. Now Willow can pursue music again. I told her I'd be more than happy to go find one of the record producers I coerced not to sign her and get them to change their mind, but she said no." They looked at one another.

"That's right. Because I'd rather know I got a contract because I deserved it." She leaned down and kissed him.

"What are you going to do with yourself while Willow's out chasing fortune and fame?" Zoriana questioned.

"Delaney and Evie have agreed to move here since they are Protectors and even though there are no threats to Willow, the Oracle must always have a security detail… With those two up here I'm going to employee them and have them help me start a high end security company." He looked over at their daughter. "And Lily's gonna help, aren't you sweetie?" She babbled excitedly in response.

"When do you guys leave?" Willow looked between Phaedra and Max while she asked the question.

"What?" Eli raised his eyebrows and looked at the two of them in confusion.

Phaedra looked at Max and smirked. "I told you she knew. She's an Oracle. She probably saw it in a vision."

Max looked at her while continuing to bounce Lily on his knee. "Is that how you know?"

"Sorry." Willow cupped her hand over her mouth and giggled.

"And Zoriana and I are the last two to know this big secret?" Eli tried to act like he was pouting.

"I'm afraid it's just you." Zoriana teased him.

Everyone laughed.

"I'm sorry, baby." Willow kissed him on the cheek as she chuckled.

"So, I'm losing my best friend and fellow Protectors to what?" Eli looked between the two of them again.

Phaedra explained what they'd just signed up for. "We've been asked by the Congress of Supernatural Beings to head up a task force that will investigate supernatural incidents and occurrences around the world. It will act kind of like an FBI or CIA branch of the government now that the Congress has decided to make supernaturals known to the whole world."

"So they're really going through with it, huh? Telling the whole world about us?" Eli ruminated over Congress' decision to out supernaturals whether everyone was in agreement or not. "Well get ready for the shit to hit the fan. You guys are going to have your work cut out for you..." He smiled at Phaedra. "I hate to lose you, but they couldn't have picked a better person for the job."

"Don't go getting all weepy on me, Elias. You know we'll still drop in from time to time." Phaedra stood and glanced around. "Where's that apple brandy I brought over here as a housewarming gift. I think we could all use a drink."

Zoriana helped find glasses, once Phaedra located the bottle of alcohol.

"What about you Zoriana?" Willow looked at her.

"I'm retiring. Alistair and I are going to go travel, but I'll be around to visit this cutie as often as I can... Lily Mathilda Walker." She squeezed the little girl's hand.

A couple hours later, as they sat around, laughing and joking, Willow couldn't help but think how fortunate she was. For a girl, who started out life alone, after her mother died, she was now surrounded by an abundance of family, friends and most of all...love.

***

Later that night, as they lay in bed together in their new house, with Lily nestled between them; Eli looked at her and caressed her cheek. "Baby, do you still think about the life you could have had if I hadn't sabotaged it?"

Looking down at Lily, her little butt in the air as she slept between them, she grinned. When she looked back up into his eyes, she thought about all that they'd been through together and knew she would gladly do it all over again if it brought her right back here to her family. It was nice to be back in Nashville again... and yeah, it would be nice to get a recording contract, but she was okay if it never happened because she had the two of them.

"I rather like singing for an audience of two these days."

He smiled brightly at her and leaned across their sleeping daughter and kissed her. When he pulled back she looked at him sexily. "Now Wizard, when are you going to say Abracadabra and show me some of your magical moves." She giggled as he picked up Lily and got out of bed and put her in her crib.

When he got back in bed, he pulled her flush against his body. "Abracadabra, baby. Open up those sexy legs for me." He growled at her, which sent her off into peals of laughter, right before he silenced her with a hungry kiss.

***

STAY TUNED IN 2020!
This isn't the end for some of these characters!
Some characters will be getting their own spin-off
series: Max & Phaedra will be getting a series +
Katana will get her own series. Plus, I will be
checking in on Willow & Eli from time to time with
a short story or novella or two. Join my newsletter
below to stay in the know.

The Oracle Chronicles Series
https://www.moniboyce.com/series/oraclechronicles

Keep up with Moni's releases by joining her newsletter!
moniboyce.com

Also By Moni Boyce:
Redemption of the Heart

TRANSLATIONS

LATIN:

Attineo hic venefica de effectio magia.
Keep this witch from performing magic.

Reconcinno.
Repair

Inficio hic cruor. Exhaurio vis et crour de hic lamia. Verto corpus ad cineresco. Interficio!
Poison this blood. Drain the strength and blood from this vampire. Turn his body to ash. Kill.

Maiorum, audierit a senioribus. Ibi unus dignabilis ut habeo tuus daemon et potestatem spirituum. Imbuo illum apud eius hereditatem et quod primogenita vendidisset. Permitto illum audite tuus voces, percipio tuus impes fluit apud eius venas, ita quod autem habet vos apud illum semper.
Ancestors, hear the Elders. There is one worthy to have your spirits and powers. Imbue him with his heritage, his

birthright. Let him hear your voices, feel your energy flowing through his veins, so he may have you with him always.

Mali spiritus, consurgetis de insidiis et ipsum relevare.
Evil spirit, come out of hiding and reveal thyself.

GREEK:

Eíste i kóri tis mitéras sas.
You are your mother's daughter.

ACKNOWLEDGMENTS

First and foremost, I want to thank God, because without him none of this would be possible. I'm grateful to have the time and means to do something I love and I love storytelling. I've enjoyed specifically telling Willow and Eli's stories and sharing their journeys with all of you. It's been so much fun. By no means is this the end of this world. I have many more character's stories to delve into so please sign up for my newsletter to be updated.

I want to acknowledge and thank my family and friends for always supporting and encouraging me. My parents and my sisters are so supportive and encouraging. I appreciate their understanding when I tell them I must disappear into my writing cave for a while. It means a lot to have them in my corner. Special thanks to my sister, Desi, for being reading and helping to catch things I might have missed, be it grammar, plot points. I appreciate your lawyer brain asking the tough questions.

If you're interested in seeing visuals of how I saw the characters or even how I envisioned Willow's wedding dress you can check out my Pinterest board for The Oracle Chronicles on my Pinterest https://www.pinterest.com/moniboyce.

Again, I just want to send a huge shout out to Mallory Rock who designed the covers for the series because she did a phenomenal job. They are beautiful and I get tons of compliments on them.

I also want to thank all of my writer pals, because having a community of other writers to commiserate with during the writing process is invaluable. It means a lot to have people to turn to that get how crazy writing can make you.

A really big thank you and shout out to all of my readers. You guys rock for buying and reading this book, and the series. I truly hope you haven't been disappointed and that you had a satisfying ending for Willow and Eli's characters. You will see them pop up again in other character's stories. I hope you will check out my other books. I know there are lots of ways you could spend your money and your time and it means a lot that you chose to spend it reading my book(s). You have my gratitude.

Disclaimer: Some Scottish town names used in the book are made up.

What Did You Think of Divined: The Oracle Chronicles?

First of all, thank you for purchasing this book **Divined: The Oracle Chronicles**. *I know you could have picked any number of books to read, but you picked this book and for that I am extremely grateful.*

I hope that it added value and quality to your everyday life. If so, it would be really nice if you could share this book with your friends and family by posting to Facebook and Twitter.

If you enjoyed this book and found some benefit in reading this, I'd like to hear from you and hope that you could take some time to post a review. Your feedback and support will help me as an author to greatly improve my writing craft for future projects and make this book even better.

I want you, the reader, to know that your review is very important and so, if you'd like to **leave a review**, *all you have to do is go to Amazon, Goodreads or Bookbub or the site where you purchased the book. I wish you all the best in your future success!*

About the Author

 Moni Boyce is a writer, filmmaker, poet and author of contemporary and paranormal romance. She spent the last fifteen years working in the film industry and now creates characters of her own and brings them to life on the page. Moni has ghostwritten romance novellas and novels for over a year now and decided to put some of her own creations out in the world. She considers herself a bookworm, film buff, foodie, music lover and an avid world traveler having visited 33 countries and counting. She lives a bit of a nomadic life, but considers Los Angeles home. Which is the subject of her first travel book: Greater Than A Tourist – Los Angeles, California: 50 Travel Tips From A Local. Learn more about her at www.moniboyce.com

http://www.facebook.com/MoniBoyceWrites
http://www.twitter.com/MoniBoyce
http://www.bookbub.com/authors/moni-boyce
http://www.goodreads.com/moniboyce
http://www.instagram.com/moniboyce